"Retaliation is a vital book that will fly off the shelves in any "urban" library and your problem will be how to find more books for your young people who want to read…" **Amy Cheney, Librarian, Alameda County Library, Juvenile Hall Literacy**

"It wasn't until I read Retaliation that I thought about my life and where I'd end up if I did something that I would regret. Your book helped my sister and me. It allowed us to see a bigger picture…" **Saquota R., Actual Teen Reader**

"It's important for the youth to read Retaliation so that they can see what could happen if they make the wrong decisions…" **Officer Tinsley, 19-Year Veteran, Metropolitan Police Department, Washington, DC**

"Your book Retaliation really spoke to me because it reminds me of my life now… Thank you for writing this book. You're a great author." **Jasmine C., Actual Teen**

"Finally a novel that is a great read and one a parent can safely pass to a teenager…" **Locksie, ARC Book Club**

"I read the entire book in one sitting. I really didn't want to put it down. I'm sure that our young ladies [at our school] will find the story and all its parts quite interesting…" **Leslie Simms-Holston, MA Certified School Psychologist**

Praise for The Blueprint for My Girls

"The Blueprint for My Girls is an inspirational book that does exactly what it promises: shows the reader how to become the woman she aspires to be." -- **Rosalind Wiseman, author of *Queenbees and Wannabes***

"Yasmin Shiraz answers the questions the way that we all wish we could have had them answered for us when we were growing up." --**BET.com**

"I love Yasmin Shiraz for having the courage to tell her real life stories." --**India.Arie**, singer/songwriter

"Shiraz is tough but right on. I wish I had read this book when I was 18."--**Mothering Magazine**

"Yasmin Shiraz has written an excellent book filled with everyday wisdom and common sense advice."
--**Right On! Magazine**

"...a copy of [The Blueprint For My Girls] which should be in every teenage girl's room."
--**LatinoLA.com**

"The author's blueprints will become meaningful imprints for self-determination and empowerment on your journey through womanhood." --- **Dr. Gwendolyn Goldsby Grant, Psychologist, Advice Columnist ESSENCE MAGAZINE, and author of THE BEST KIND OF LOVING**

"I respect Yasmin Shiraz for being so brave in writing this book and sharing her emotions." -- **Kyla Pratt, actress**

RETALIATION

ALSO BY YASMIN SHIRAZ

Adult Fiction
Exclusive: A Novel
Privacy: A Novel

Young Adult Non-Fiction
The Blueprint for My Girls: How to Build A Life Full of Courage, Determination & Self-Love

The Blueprint for My Girls In Love: 99 Rules for Dating, Relationships & Intimacy

The Blueprint Guide to Motivation & Success: Identify, Focus On & Achieve Your Goals!

RETALIATION

A Novel

By

Yasmin Shiraz

ISBN: 978-0-9718174-3-2

Library of Congress Control Number: 2007931127

For more information:
Rolling Hills Press, LLC
PO Box 220053, Chantilly, VA 20153

Email: **yshiraz@yasminshiraz.net**

www.yasminshiraz.net www.rhpress.com

For the families that live through violence infecting their schools and neighborhoods, that have yet to see a social intervention rid their communities of this poison.

Author's Note:

In Washington, DC, groups that conduct themselves in the same manner as gangs on the West Coast call themselves crews. The term "crew" doesn't have the criminal association as "gang" and therefore many of us in the Washington, DC area don't believe that we have a gang problem. It is a great illustration of the power of words. However, children of the inner city do not separate their fear by the name of the group that caused it.

The Letter

Miss Yasmin,

You visited my school last month in Southeast, DC. I was the girl sitting way in the back with long braids. You probably don't remember me. I didn't say one word during your whole speech. But since you gave us your MySpace address, I checked you out and decided to connect. All that stuff you were saying about choosing the life you want and being positive, it sounds good, but it doesn't work around here. In my 'hood we have people fighting that live two blocks from each other. I live in the Deuce Trés (23rd Street) and we're at war with Deuce Five (25th Street.) If somebody from Deuce Five sees someone from Deuce Trés, a fight can jump off right on the spot. Hearing guns pop off is an every day, every hour situation. I used to have friends in like 3rd grade that lived in the Deuce Five area, but now if I see one of them, they act like they don't know me, and I gotta act all rumble tumble or they'll try to punk me. And that's just when I get home. At school, girls are fighting each other over boys, what you look like and what you wearing. I've always tried to be cool with everybody. Ugly girls, pretty girls, best dressed and bummy, they've all been my friends--until nine days ago, when I was coming out the mini-mart and this girl and two of her friends jumped me. I don't know why they jumped me, not really. I would tell you, but it'd make this letter too long. My point is you said we could choose the life we wanted, and I didn't choose to be jumped. I didn't choose to live in a neighborhood where people are dying everyday. But that's exactly where I am. If you say we can choose our life, you gotta help me choose something different. 'Cause right now, I'm carrying a switchblade everywhere I go. And if the wrong person steps to me, I'm choosing death- for my enemy.

Your girl,

Tashera

Chapter 1

For the latter part of the day at Marion Barry High School, Tashera Odom dreamt about an oatmeal crème pie and a grape soda. When the school bell rang, she couldn't wait to get on the bus and jet to the store for her coveted snack. Her trademark invisible braids – with a red braid in the front and all of them in a ponytail – bounced as much as she did as she walked into Meha's Mini-Mart on R Street in SE, Washington, DC. When Tashera reached the counter, Mr. Cho asked her about her family.

"Shee Shee, you here by yourself today? No brother with you today?"

"Nah, I'm rolling solo. But I had to get my snack on." Tashera's brother Khalil was confined to a wheelchair and stayed at home until she returned from school. He mostly played video games all day. Tashera knew he'd be mad that she didn't get him before she walked to the store, but her cravings didn't want her to go home first.

As Mr. Cho took her money, Tashera heard loud music outside. She turned toward the front door and saw an old car, like a Chevy or a Ford with dark tinted windows.

"Those windows are so dark. They'll mess around and get arrested if the police catch 'em," Tashera said. Mr. Cho just looked at Tashera and nodded.

Tashera exited the store, turned up the volume on her iPod and took a left up the street. Her house in Barry Farms was a short five-block walk away. At the end of the first block, the car with the tinted windows began to follow her. Tashera cut through an open parking lot and the car pulled in front of her.

"What the…?" Tashera said almost dropping her oatmeal crème pie from her hand. Three girls in hoodies and black sunglasses jumped out of the car and surrounded Tashera who took her ear buds off and put them deep into her jeans pocket.

"Yeah, we got you now," the short girl said. The girls circled Tashera, who tried to cut out of the circle, but the biggest girl out of the crew kept pushing her back.

Tashera stared at the girls' faces. One of the girls looked vaguely familiar, but she couldn't remember where she'd seen her. *I gotta find a way outta this*, Tashera thought. *I gotta come up with an escape route*. Tashera had run track from sixth grade through eighth grade. She'd even competed in the state finals. The three girls, one tall and muscular, one short and dumpy, and the other tall and slim wouldn't really have a chance if Tashera started running. No way she'd let them catch her.

"I don't know you," she said. "You got me confused with somebody else."

"Nah, it's you. Everybody says it's you, now you gon' get yours."

Tashera dropped her bag with her soda and her brother's pork rinds inside. She tugged at the straps on her book bag. She didn't want her book bag falling when she bolted the scene. She decided it would be easier to knock the skinny girl down and run the rest of the way home because the two heavier girls wouldn't be able to catch up. As the clock struck three in her head, Tashera ran toward the skinny girl as hard as she could, throwing a hard elbow toward the girl's rib cage. The shorter girl, almost foreseeing Tashera's move, stuck her stubby leg in front of Tashera, and they watched as she fell face first to the ground. All three of the girls took turns kicking Tashera in the back, legs, and belly.

"You ain't gon' be able to have no babies now," the big girl shouted and kicked Tashera as hard as she could just below her belly button.

Tashera passed out.

****

Paramedic Ashe Thurgood had been visiting his elderly grandmother when he looked out the window and saw three girls kicking and yelling at a girl who lay motionless on the ground. He picked up his cell phone and called police though he didn't believe that they would come to Barry Farms in a rush to save a girl who had been jumped. He grabbed his medical bag and ran through the parking lot.

"Y'all need to step away from her," Ashe yelled as he flashed his paramedic's badge. The three girls looked at him. Tashera let out a moan on the ground.

"What you gonna do with that?" The big girl asked while looking at Ashe's badge.

"Nothing. But I'm a fifth degree black belt, and if you don't get back in your vehicle and get away from this girl, I'll be forced to subdue you."

"Calia, let's go. Let's go," the skinny girl said to her crew.

"Don't say my name," uttered the big girl.

Ashe kneeled down and felt around Tashera's abdomen. He could tell at least two of her ribs were broken. He picked up his phone, ready to dial 911. Instead, he called one of his friends who was still at work driving an ambulance and told him to come pick them up. He hoped that the girl's internal bleeding wouldn't kill her before the ambulance got there.

****

Khalil Odom wheeled himself to the window in the living room and waited for Tashera. Though he was five years older than her, Khalil liked spending time with his 17-year-old sister. Besides, he needed her. The area along his spine where the bullet had entered was especially sore, and his little sister Shera would put a heating pad on it to make the pain go away.

Every time that pain resonated, Khalil thought back to his life just a few short years ago. Four years ago, he was 2nd lieutenant of the Deuce Trés crew. In a robbery gone bad, Khalil was shot by a part-time security guard who was determined to prevent the neighborhood electronics store from getting robbed. It was supposed to be an easy inside job. Darren had sweet-talked a lady supervisor at Eddie's Electronics to give him a copy of the key that unlocked the bars and gates in the front of the store. After the gates opened, the Deuce Trés crew had planned to go into the store and take at least three flat screen televisions. But the lady supervisor failed to mention that Eddie's Electronics had an undercover security guard patrolling the store every thirty minutes. When Khalil attempted to load his television into the trunk of their Escalade, the security guard started shooting. The back window of the truck shattered and so did Khalil's spine.

****

Khalil had gone to therapy for the past four years and every doctor told him that he'd never walk again. They also told him that he wouldn't be in any pain, but as a person who'd been paralyzed from the waist down, Khalil felt pain in his back every day that he opened his eyes.

Khalil took out a cell phone that was strapped into a pouch on his chair. He didn't normally worry about his sister, but today his hand began to shake around the time that Tashera would have been home. He called Tashera's phone and it just rang. Khalil hung up and went back over to the video game console. He shut the TV off just as his phone rang. He looked at the Caller ID. It was Tashera.

"Where you been all day?" he said when he answered the phone. "You know we're supposed to go to the store."

"Sir, I'm with the girl who had this phone in her backpack. She's unconscious. We're on the way to Greater Southeast Community Hospital. She was jumped by a group of girls. A couple of her ribs are broken and she's bleeding internally."

"No," Khalil screamed and threw the phone against the television. "This can't be happening," Khalil cried.

Chapter 2

Sheila Odom worked as an administrative assistant at Laurel Hospital. Every morning before her two kids woke up, she sat on the metro for her twenty-five-minute commute. She hated her job. For years she trained other workers who because they had college degrees or no criminal record, became her supervisors. It happened all the time. She made one mistake when she was a teenager, and she's had to pay for it her entire life.

It wasn't even a mistake she started or provoked. The day after her 18th birthday, Sheila and a couple of her friends went to a carnival in Alexandria, Virginia. They were getting on the rides and talking to cute guys who winked at them. One guy, a Puerto-Rican by the name of Carlos stepped to Sheila.

"You are so fine," he told her.

"Whatever," Sheila said and walked away.

Carlos followed behind.

"Why don't you give me your number? I'll call you."

"Nah, that's okay. I don't live around here, so I ain't trying to have a long distance relationship."

"Dag. You're gonna shoot down your soul mate like that? We're meant to be together."

Sheila looked at Carlos. He was about five-foot-ten with short black hair and long black eye lashes. He blinked at her, and she reached down into her purse. Before she could get a piece of paper or pen out of her bag, a girl jumped in between Sheila and Carlos and started yelling in Spanish. Sheila couldn't understand a word the girl was

8

saying until she pointed at Sheila and said, "Beech." Sheila's friends stood around and had begun to roll their necks and point their fingers.

"I know you ain't gonna let her call you out of your name," Sheila's friend Tilly said.

The Puerto Rican girl's friends strolled over, and before Sheila could think straight, she and her three friends were outranked by the seven Puerto Rican girls who stood before them, ready to bring it on. Sheila looked around, and Carlos was nowhere to be found.

"Beech, if you want my man, you come and take my man," the girl who had been yelling at Carlos said.

Tilly whispered to Sheila, "There are seven of them and only four of us. But, I got a switchblade in my pocket. Ima give it to you 'cause if you cut the girl with all the mouth, the rest of these hussies will go running."

Sheila had never handled a knife outside of the kitchen when Tilly gave her the blade. With reluctance Sheila took the knife, felt her thumb along the blade release mechanism, and before Carlos' girl uttered another word, the knife was up at her cheek ready to write, "Hola chica!" The girl's friends saw Sheila's blade and started to back away.

"What you got to say now, chili con carne?" Sheila asked with a smirk on her face. The girl stood, her eyes wide, speechless. Just then, Tilly pushed Sheila from behind and the knife jabbed into the Puerto Rican girl's neck. Instantly, one of her friends started screaming, and police swarmed Sheila like they were on a presidential detail.

In a flash, Sheila found herself thrown upon the ground, handcuffed, and pushed into the back of a police car.

For a mistake, for something she never planned to do, Sheila spent three weeks in the Alexandria city jail before she was sentenced to six months in a juvenile facility and two years of probation.

****

Sheila sat at her desk and looked at a picture of Khalil and Tashera. It seemed like a long time ago. Khalil was still standing, and Tashera had allowed Sheila to do her hair that day--two things that never happened anymore. She often became sad when she thought about her only son not being able to walk. But she had reasoned that he had been a part of a gang, and anything can happen to young men in those circumstances. She ran her finger over the outline of Tashera's face. She'd go crazy if anything ever happened to Tashera. The girl wasn't perfect, but she was the closest thing to it. Just then Sheila looked over at her phone. She smiled to herself when she saw Tashera's number flash on the phone's screen.

"What's happening baby?" Sheila asked.

"Ma'am, I'm sorry to call you under these circumstances."

"Who is this? Where is Tashera?"

"Ma'am, I found your daughter being beaten in a parking lot. We're at Greater Southeast Community Hospital. You need to come as quickly as you can."

Sheila grabbed her purse and left. She didn't bother telling anyone where she'd gone. She didn't care if they'd miss her; she had to go and save her baby.

****

On the metro, Sheila kept wondering who could have wanted to fight her daughter. Overall, Tashera was quiet girl who tried to keep to herself. Sheila knew that Tashera didn't have any enemies. For the past year or so, Tashera had become the "hot high school hairstylist." She was doing so many girls' heads that she sent Sheila to a full day at the spa for Mother's Day, paid for it all in cash, and took her out to dinner afterwards. Tashera was the perfect daughter. "Why did this happen to Tashera," Sheila mouthed out loud. She thought about Tashera's angry customers, people who could have been mad at her for taking their hair out. Tashera didn't have any of those. Maybe some girls were jealous of her because of how she dressed. Sheila doubted that. Tashera would spend her money on her mother and on her brother's video games and shoes that he never wore the tread off of, but she didn't buy a lot of expensive gear for herself. Sheila recalled talking to Tashera about her spending.

"You know," she had told Tashera, "you work hard. You can spend some money on yourself."

"Nah, I'm okay. I'm saving it."

"Saving it for what?"

"You never know what comes up. I want to have it for a rainy day or whatever."

"Girl, you act like you're 100 years old sometimes."

Sheila and Tashera just laughed.

The only new thing in Tashera's life was that guy that she'd been hanging around and calling all of a sudden. Sheila remembered Tashera telling her that he was the best player on the basketball team or something like that. Sheila's blood began to boil. If she knew anything from her past, she knew that a girl would fight someone to the death over a boy. The metro door chimed, and Sheila got off at the Greater Southeast Community Hospital's metro stop, determination blazing in her eyes. She knew two things for certain: she would make sure her daughter was okay, and she would make whoever did this pay.

****

After basketball practice, Ahmed Warner called Tashera's cell phone, and it went straight into voice mail. After fourth period, Tashera told him to call her as soon as practice ended. He'd hoped that she'd let him hang out over her house. Lately a lot of the girls at school had been circulating rumors saying that Ahmed was cheating on Tashera behind her back. None of it was true. But Ahmed tried to pay extra attention to Tashera these days to reassure her.

Ahmed decided to wait a few minutes at the front of the school before he headed in the opposite direction of Tashera's house. Before Ahmed could sit on the front steps and pull out his iPod, his best friend Mike came running from the gym's side door.

"Yo, Ahmed," Mike said, slightly out of breath, "have you been able to reach Tashera?"

"Not yet. Why? What's up?"

"I just heard some bad stuff happened to her."

"What are you talking about?"

"Word on the street is some girls jumped her after school."

Ahmed grabbed his cell phone and called Tashera's house again.

"Man, can you drop me by Tashera's house real quick?"

Mike nodded, and he and Ahmed ran to his silver Accord. Ahmed never raised his hand to hit a girl, but if his ex-girlfriend and her clique hurt Tashera, he didn't know how he'd keep his anger under control.

Chapter 3

Tashera lay in her hospital bed with bandages wrapped around her head and abdomen. She opened her eyes every now and then and grimaced with pain. She remembered the girls in the hoodies. The short one looked so familiar to her. She attempted to recall where she knew her from. Nothing came to her cloud-filled brain.

Tashera had been getting threatening notes at her locker for the past couple of weeks. Notes that said STAY AWAY FROM AHMED. Tashera didn't know who slipped the notes into her locker. She couldn't believe anybody was really that petty. She never sweated Ahmed or broke her neck to try to be with him; in fact, Ahmed begged for her phone number, followed her around school, and asked her to wear his platinum chain. Anybody who told her to stay away from Ahmed should have first told Ahmed to stay away from her.

Tashera noticed Ahmed for the first time seven months ago while she sat in the cafeteria.

Ahmed came up to her table and said, "I want to get to know you, Tashera. Can I sit here?"

"How do you know my name?" she asked.

"Everybody knows you."

"Wrong. I stay under the radar."

"That's why I know you. You're the only fly girl in this whole school that ain't in everybody's business."

Tashera's smiled 'cause it was true. Outside of doing hair and getting her homework done, Tashera didn't care about people and their business.

13

"You got a boyfriend?" Ahmed asked.

"That's kinda personal for our first conversation."

"I want to know if I have a chance."

Tashera's light brown eyes danced at the idea of her having a boyfriend. She recalled all of her clients—girls whose hair she braided—they all had boyfriends and stories about their boyfriends and heartbreak about their boyfriends. Tashera hadn't even had a first kiss.

"Well, do you?" Ahmed asked again, breaking into Tashera's thoughts.

"Nah, I don't have a boyfriend," she replied. "I don't have time for people who aren't serious. You don't look like you're serious to me. You look like you're some kind of playboy with a bunch of chicks on the side. I'm not trying to be your next chick or the ex-chick. I'm busy."

With that, Tashera walked away from Ahmed and left him sitting in the cafeteria rejected by a girl for the first time in his popular athlete life. Ahmed smiled as he watched Tashera strut out of the cafeteria as if she owned the whole school.

****

Khalil's neighbor, Mr. Johnson, dropped him off at the hospital. After Khalil found where Tashera was resting, he made his way to her room.

When he entered her room, he saw that her face had been bandaged, her lip had been split, and one of her eyes was swollen. He came to her bedside and held her hand.

"Shera, you're going to be okay."

Tashera opened her eyes and barely smiled.

"The people who did this to you? I'm going to get them."

Tashera closed her eyes.

Khalil wheeled himself as close as he could to Tashera's bed. He saw all of Tashera's cuts, bruises and swelling up close. For the first time, he knew what it felt like to see someone you love in so much pain.

When he was still walking and using drugs, Khalil and his Deuce Trés crew robbed people, fought other gangs, and stole cars. One time they followed a couple that had recently exited a movie theater in Georgetown. It was a late night, the guy wore an impressive gold chain, and the couple had parked their car on a dark street away from the theater's main parking lot. Khalil grabbed the girl and covered her mouth while Darren and Nathan "Nut-Nut" Briggs pounced on the guy, yanking his chain from his neck.

"Give me all your money," Darren said to the guy whose face had already begun to bleed.

"And I want those Gucci loafers. They look to be my size," Nut-Nut said to the guy as he took his shoes off of his feet.

Deuce Trés were used to Nut-Nut saying the craziest things in the midst of a robbery or carjacking.

Khalil whispered to the lady, "There's an ATM right around that corner. You and I are gonna walk over there and you're going to take out $500 dollars and give it to me. If you don't do it, we'll kill your boyfriend here."

The lady started crying.

"Stop crying! Let's start walking now. If you even think of screaming, I'm going to stomp a hole in you myself."

The lady lowered her head and walked to the ATM.

Khalil took the money as the ATM spit out the twenty-dollar bills. He walked the lady back to her wounded boyfriend and their car. And then out of nowhere, he punched her in the eye. The lady fell to the ground.

"Dang," Darren said, chuckling. "She took that like a man."

"I don't want her to ever think about going to the police or telling anybody what I look like," Khalil said. "It was a hit she'll never forget."

It was also a hit Khalil knew looked identical to the shiner that was decorated around his baby sister's eye.

****

Dr. Elliot entered Tashera's room just as Sheila arrived.

"Oh no, no, no," Sheila cried.

"Are you her mother?" Dr. Elliot asked as Khalil rolled his wheelchair over to be at his mother's side.

Sheila nodded and sat at a chair pulled next to Tashera's bed.

"I know her face looks bad, but the swelling will go down in a couple of days. The fight exhausted her."

"What fight?" Sheila said, hysteria bubbling along the surface of her words. "She was jumped. This wasn't a fair one!"

"Ma'am, I'm just trying to say that I don't believe there has been any permanent damage to her face or head. But in some other areas..."

"What do you mean other areas?"

"Your daughter was bleeding internally in her abdomen, and it was very close to her uterus and her reproductive organs."

"Are you telling me she won't be able to have children?"

"No. But it's really too early to tell."

Sheila shook her head.

"The girls who did this are going to pay," Sheila said. "This ain't right. Somebody's gonna die for hurting my baby."

"Ma. Ma," Tashera mumbled.

16

Sheila looked up at Tashera's battered face.

"Ma, don't cry."

Sheila felt a burning in her chest hot enough to turn charcoal gray. Tashera was always worrying about somebody else. She'd rather concern herself with her mother crying than focus on the pain she must have been feeling.

"Do you know who did this to you?" Sheila asked.

Tashera shook her head no.

Sheila quietly started sobbing again.

"Ma, by the end of the week, I will find out who did this to her. I still have respect in the streets."

Khalil's words brought a tightening around Sheila's heart.

Sheila looked at her son. He was handsome. His skin, the color of an apple dipped in caramel with eyes to match. If it weren't for him being paralyzed, Khalil would have made Sheila a grandmother by now. But drugs, violence, and the lure of the street took the promise of her son's life right from him. The wheelchair was just a cruel bonus to the sentence Khalil received due to his fast living.

Khalil made a choice to become one with the streets.

Tashera did not. In Sheila's mind, whoever jumped Tashera was trying to take her life from her.

"I will never let that happen." Sheila said out loud.

She turned to Khalil and said, "There are some things a mother has to take care of. Somebody violated your sister, and I will handle it as her mother and as her protector."

Sheila knew that whoever did this to Tashera would be bragging at school. She would talk to some of Tashera's clients, and it would only be a matter of time before she found out whose head she'd have to crack.

Chapter 4

Ahmed tossed and turned all night. He woke up intermittently to look at his cell phone. He had hoped that Tashera would call and end his nightmare.

At midnight, he received a call from an unknown number.

"Hello?" he answered.

"We got your girlfriend."

His phone died.

Ahmed sat up in his bed. He didn't know the voice on the phone. It sounded like tons of girls—tons of girls who he'd given his number. Before he started dating Tashera, he tried to date as many girls as possible. There were girls who'd perform oral on him on their first date, girls who would have sex with him whenever and wherever he wanted, and girls who believed any lie that he told them—especially when he said, "I'll call you tomorrow," after he got all that he wanted from them. At seventeen, Ahmed had girls lining up for him—until Tashera.

On their first date, Ahmed met Tashera at the movie theater at Pentagon City Mall. Ahmed suggested they connect an hour before the movie started. Ahmed wanted to hold hands with Tashera before the movie with hopes that would lead to some extra-closeness inside the theater. But Tashera wasn't having it. She showed up ten minutes before the movie started, just in time for her to tell him, "I'll buy my own popcorn and snacks. But since you invited me to this date, you can pay for my ticket."

All throughout the movie, Ahmed tried to lean on Tashera. Tashera would say to him, "Are you sleepy or something? Maybe you should call your mom to come pick you up."

"I'm not sleepy. I'm just trying to…"

"Tryna what? Treat me like your groupies? I'm no groupie, Ahmed. You need to check your facts."

After the movie, Tashera didn't speak to Ahmed for the rest of the evening. Ahmed was used to girls making a big deal over him because he was a popular athlete. He didn't know how to deal with Tashera. He wasn't used to girls standing up for themselves or standing up to him.

Ahmed's cell phone rang again.

"Hello?" he said. "Who is this?"

"It's me baby," Tashera said. "I miss you."

"What's going on? You sound tired."

"I am. I'm in the hospital. I got jumped today."

Ahmed felt his heart stop.

"Which hospital?"

"Greater Southeast. But visiting hours are over."

"Not for me. I'll see you in a little while."

Ahmed called Mike, put on a sweat suit, and waited for Mike to take him to the hospital.

****

Tashera sat up in her bed. Her back and sides felt like a tractor-trailer had run over her. She knew she should have been resting, but Ahmed would be there any minute, and she wanted to fix herself up a little before then. As she stepped out of the bed, she held on to its sides. She hardly had the strength to stand up let alone walk anywhere. She managed to hobble over to the closet. She looked inside and saw her book bag. She was so glad. She kept her favorite lip-glosses in her bag. She refused to see Ahmed with chapped, cracked lips. She dragged her book bag along the floor. She stopped in the bathroom and was shocked to see her swollen face. Her left eye was practically shut.

"He's going to think I'm totally ugly," Tashera said and cried. Holding on to the edge of the sink, Tashera began to feel weak. As she felt her weight shifting backwards, Ahmed came up from behind and lifted her to her bed. Tashera wanted to smile, but her face wouldn't let her.

****

Ahmed tucked Tashera in and bit his lip at the sight of her bruised face. He was not prepared for what had happened to her. As his left hand held on to hers, his right hand remain in a clinched fist.

Who likes me so much that they would hurt Tashera so badly, Ahmed thought.

The life of a popular athlete is supposed to be filled with girls, fun, scholarships, and easy-going relationships with the teachers. It's not supposed to be about violence.

Ahmed's family moved to Washington, DC, from Charlotte, NC, because his mother would make more money with her government job in DC. The move had nothing to do with his interest in the area. In fact, if he ever told the truth, he'd tell people that he hated the area. He hated the shootings. He hated the jealousy. He hated girls who fought other girls over boys who were not even really thinking about them. He hated the cliques-the crews that you hung around because it was what you were supposed to do. In their school, there was a thug-clique, Deuce-Trés gang clique, the jock clique, the nerd-clique, the best-dressed clique, and on and on. There were more cliques in the public school system than a hooker in high heels walking the boardwalk.

Ahmed hated cliques, and he feared that a girl that liked him was behind the attack on Tashera. Who else could have called his cell phone? Ahmed looked at Tashera who had fallen asleep. She didn't look the same, but she still was beautiful.

"How could a girl to do this to another girl?" he asked himself as he looked at the gash above Tashera's eyebrow.

His cell phone rang; he read UNKNOWN NUMBER on his Caller ID and answered.

"She ain't fly no more, is she?"

"Who is this?" Ahmed yelled.

"What does Medusa look like now?"

Ahmed heard chuckles in the background. Then he heard somebody say, "Calia, hang up. My mom is comin'."

Ahmed repeated the name "Calia" over in his head. Calia was the friend of a girl who really liked him.

"I bet they did this," Ahmed said and put his head in his hands. He didn't want Tashera to hurt anymore than she was already, but could he keep it a secret that he thought he knew who attacked her? Would she dump him if she found out that a chickenhead that he used to get freaky with was the one who hurt her so badly? He never hated his reckless sexual behavior until that moment.

Chapter 5

Sheila returned to the hospital at five in the morning. She called and left a message with her job supervisor that a family emergency had occurred with her daughter and that she would not be in for a couple of days. She wanted to stay overnight in the hospital with Tashera but decided that she still had to keep an eye on Khalil; she wanted to make sure his back wasn't bothering him.

Tashera had been sitting up in the hospital bed when Sheila walked into her room. The swelling in Tashera's face had gone down considerably.

"You look so much better today," Sheila said. "How you feeling?"

"My face itches under these bandages and my ribs hurt. Other than that, I'm okay, I guess."

Sheila patted Tashera's hand.

"Hello, can I come in?" Ashe, the paramedic asked as he stood outside Tashera's door.

"Who are you?" Sheila asked ready to pounce on the intruder.

"I found her yesterday."

"Thank You. Thank you," Sheila got up and hugged Ashe. "I spoke with you on the phone. I'm her mother, Sheila Odom." Sheila sat at the edge of Tashera's bed.

"How's your progress, Miss Lady?" Ashe asked.

Tashera smiled a little and re-opened the split on her lip.

"Okay."

"Her name is Tashera," Sheila added.

"Oh. Tashera, I'm glad to see you're doing better."

Sheila leaned toward Ashe and asked, "Can I talk to you outside for a minute?"

"Sure."

Sheila stroked Tashera's forearm. "I'll be right back, baby." She handed Tashera a few tissues from the box on the nightstand. "For your lip."

Ashe followed Sheila out into the hall.

As soon as the door closed behind them, she turned to Ashe and asked, "When you found her, was she by herself?"

"No and I'm willing to make a report to the police."

"Who was there?"

"This is information that needs to be taken to the police."

"Do you see the police in here trying to protect my daughter?"

Ashe just looked at Sheila.

"Listen Sir," Sheila said and stepped closer to Ashe. "We'll report everything we know to the police, but it makes sense to me to get as much information as I can so when I go to the police they're not just looking at me crazy. You know how they do that."

Ashe nodded. He knew that sometimes the less education, money, power, or influence that a person had when they walked into a police station, the worse that person could be treated.

"Where are you from?" Sheila asked.

"Southeast."

"Well, you oughta know then. If I can't give police all the information that they need, they're going to put my complaint at the bottom of the list. Remember what my

23

daughter looked like when you rescued her? Tell me that you don't want to help that girl."

Ashe looked toward Tashera's room.

"There were three girls attacking Tashera when I arrived," he finally replied.

"Three? Them wenches," Sheila said and formed a tight fist.

"Yeah and one of the girl's names was Calia."

"Thank you. I'll never forget this."

Sheila walked back into Tashera's room and sat on the bed. Tashera was busy doing a Word-Find that Sheila had brought her from home.

"Baby, I'm going down to the cafeteria and then I have to stop up to your school. I want to file an official complaint with the principal's office regarding your attack."

"Can't you stay a little longer?" Tashera asked.

Sheila paused and tried to produce a smile for her daughter.

"Okay," she said reluctantly. "I'll stay for another hour."

She wanted to get to Marion Barry High School as soon as she could. She wanted to find Calia and make sure that the girl and her crew paid for the destruction that they brought to her daughter's life.

****

Ahmed got home from the hospital in time to take a shower and catch a ride to school. At 7:15, he jumped in the car with Mike.

"How's Tashera doing?" Mike asked.

"Not well. She fell asleep as soon as I got there. She was tired, real tired."

"Does she know who did this? Did she see anybody?"

"We haven't talked about it yet."

"Why not?"

"She practically fell out as soon as I got there. You don't understand. She was hurt real bad in that fight."

"Well then, somebody gotta pay."

"And, I know who," Ahmed said.

"What do you mean?"

"Jessica and her crew did it."

"Jessica, the superfreak?"

"Yeah."

"I told you that girl was crazy," Mike said, "but you wouldn't listen."

"Not now Mike. Not now."

"How do you know it was Jessica?"

"I don't know completely, but last night some girls kept calling my cell phone saying that they did something to Tashera. Then I heard them call somebody Calia."

"And Calia is Jessica's girl," Mike said.

"Yep."

"What are you gonna do? Jessica probably went after Tashera to get you back for kicking her to the curb."

"But she went too far."

"What are you going to do?"

"I don't know yet, but I'm definitely going to do something. I have to do something."

****

The doctor had taken the bandages off of Tashera's head. Her face had already begun to heal.

"Mom, can you take my cell phone out of my backpack?" Tashera asked.

"You plan on calling somebody?"

"No, but Ahmed might call me."

"Tashera, did you see the faces of the girls who jumped you yesterday?"

"No, they had on hoodies and dark glasses."

"What would you do if you found out who did this? Would you want to fight them?"

"Yeah. It wasn't a fair one. They attacked me out of the blue for no reason. I didn't even know them."

"What if I took care of them so you didn't have to ever fight them? Would you be okay with that?"

"What do you mean?"

"Remember when the kid in K-5 kept digging in your backpack, taking your afternoon snack after you told him to stop?"

"Yeah, I remember."

"What happened to that kid?"

"You put a mouse trap in my backpack and it snapped on the boy's fingers so bad that he had to go to the hospital and get splinters on two fingers."

"Well, imagine that but much more serious."

"Mom, I can fight my own battles."

"You don't have to. Not this time."

"Mom, if we find out who did this, let's go to the police, let's go to the school; they'd get expelled."

"But will justice be done? What if the police don't do anything? What if the school doesn't do anything?"

Sheila walked over to the window and looked at all the people milling about.

"Well, if that happens," Tashera said, "I'll have to face those girls on my own."

"If that happens, the school and the police will have wished that they did their jobs."

Sheila walked over to Tashera and kissed her on the forehead and headed to Marion Barry High School to file a formal complaint against Calia and whoever were her accomplices.

Chapter 6

Ashe walked into a busy police station, to the front desk and asked to speak with Detective Stewart, one of his friends who he'd been close to since high school.

Ashe arrived in the detective's office just as the detective hung up the telephone.

"Ashy baby. What you doing in this part of town?" Detective Stewart asked and extended his hand.

"I got some business I need you to look into."

"Oh yeah, tell me more."

"Yesterday I found a girl being kicked and beaten in a parking lot behind my grandmother's spot."

"Is she still over there in Barry Farms?"

Ashe nodded. "I just happened to look out the window and I saw these girls in hoodies and dark glasses. They were kicking and yelling, moving their arms wildly and making noise."

Detective Stewart took out his tablet and began to jot down notes.

"Instinct made me grab my medical bag. I ran out the back door and headed toward them. When I got there, they were kickin' a girl who already had fallen to the ground."

"Umm. How bad was the girl hurt?"

"She got a couple of broken ribs, mostly a lot of bruises. I checked up on her in the hospital today though and her face is healing nicely. A lot of the swelling has gone down in her face though there are some dark areas around her eyes and she had to get stitches on her forehead."

Detective Stewart shook his head.

27

"What happened when you reached the scene?"

"I told the girls to back up, get in their vehicle, and get lost."

"So you have a license plate number for me then?"

"Absolutely."

Ashe reached into his pocket and gave the detective a piece of paper where he'd written the girl's tag number.

"This area isn't in my jurisdiction any more, but I'll pass this information on to Morris who'll handle it."

"Stewart, you can't do that this time. Don't you still specialize in handling gang violence?"

"Yeah."

"Well the victim, Tashera Odom is Khalil Odom's little sister."

Detective Stewart leaned back in his chair.

"You remember Khalil from when we were in high school. He was rowdy, always starting a fight. He and his boy Darren ran the Deuce Trés area like a gang. Right now, everybody says it is a gang."

"You think he'll try to retaliate? I thought he was in a wheelchair."

"He is but nothing stirs gang violence like the taste of revenge."

"Thanks for coming down here and giving me this info."

"No problem. I really want to help the girl. She doesn't seem like she's ever had a disagreement with anyone in her life, but I'm worried about Khalil. Even her mother seemed a little trigger happy."

"Her mother?"

"Yeah. Sheila Odom. She told me she was going to go to the school and jump on the principal until she found who did this."

"Did she say that?"

"Not exactly, but her point was clear. She wasn't waiting on the police to step in and punish the girls who hurt her daughter."

"I'll make this a first priority. I'll run the plates now, then over to the hospital."

"Yeah, I would. You don't have a minute to waste."

****

Sheila whipped her Camry into one of the reserved parking spaces in front of Marion Barry High School. She marched through the medal detectors and into the principal's office.

"I need to see the principal," Sheila said to a secretary who sat in the front of the office.

"Do you have an appointment?"

"No, I don't."

"Well, the principal will be in and out of meetings all day."

"Listen Miss. What's your name?"

"Miss Cannon."

"Listen Miss Cannon. My daughter was jumped yesterday while coming home from this school. Right now she's in the hospital and I'm demanding to see the principal."

"Oh, okay."

"Yeah. So I know he has a cell phone, or a pager, or a freakin' walkie-talkie. He has something for you to reach him in the case of emergency. This is one."

"Okay. What's your name, ma'am?"

"Sheila Odom."

"Ms. Odom, have a seat right there. I'll track him down for you."

"Thank you, Miss Cannon."

Sheila sat down on the short couch in the front of the office. Off to her left she saw a small stack of yearbooks on a table. She picked up the most recent yearbook and wondered if the girl Calia's picture would be inside. She started looking through all of the junior photos first. She didn't see anyone with the name Calia. She flipped through the sophomore photos and didn't see a Calia there either. Before she could get to the freshman photos, a large man, easily six-foot-six, waltzed through the door.

"Ms Odom?" the man asked as he towered over Sheila.

"Yes."

"I'm the principal, Mr. Ryland."

"Oh, glad to meet you. You look like you could be the basketball coach."

"I've heard that before. Miss Cannon told me that there's something of an emergency going on with Tashera."

"You know my daughter?"

"Well, yes and no."

"What does that mean?" Sheila asked and turned her lips up at Mr. Ryland.

"I've never had her in my office. She's not a trouble student. But, when I took over this school last year, I wanted a list of students that didn't cause trouble, were fairly academic, and looked like they had bright futures. At my school, you might imagine that wasn't a long list, but Tashera Odom was on it."

"Well her future got dark yesterday. Three hussies from your school jumped her."

"How do you know that the girls are from Barry?"

"Who else would do this?"

"I don't know."

Sheila heaved out loud. "Mr. Ryland, I'm getting frustrated with you because I sense that you're not being real with me. I was a teenager once, and I know if three girls jumped Tashera, a student with a *promising future* as you say, I know somebody in this school has been talking about

30

it. If you're on your job like you strutted in here acting like you are, you already heard that Tashera got jumped. Now am I making a lot of assumptions, or are you simply more stupid than you look?"

"We're not going to get anywhere calling names," Mr. Ryland said.

"We're not getting anywhere bs'ing each other either, which we both know you're doing."

"That's not true."

"I tried to come to you and give you the opportunity to do the right thing. Now, I see I'm going to have to go to the police and the television station and watch how they paint you as an incompetent S.O.B. So when you leave school today, you ought to start packing your bags. You won't be here long. We can't stand idiots in DC."

Sheila exited the office and marched back to her car. Inside, she steamed.

I don't know if those girls were from Barry or anywhere else, Sheila thought. *What if the girls aren't even from Tashera's school?*

****

Mr. Ryland locked his office door. He looked at the small trophy case that stood in his office. He had brought mementoes from three levels of his basketball career to showcase in his office. He had a trophy from when his team at Bowie High School won the Maryland State Basketball trophy, he had a trophy from when his team won the CIAA championship during his days at Virginia Union University, and he had his Washington Bullets jersey hanging from his days of playing for Wes Unseld. He had the trophy case in his office because he wanted his students—especially the students that came to his office for discipline issues—to know that talent could take them anywhere that they wanted to go.

Mr. Ryland turned around at his desk and looked at his incident notebook, a binder he kept filled with various problems, fights, and rumors that were happening at Barry High. Under today's date, he'd written TASHERA ODOM BEATEN BY DECALIA THOMAS, JESSICA BARNES, AND ALEXANDRA KENT. NO WITNESSES. RUMOR ONLY. He wrote the incident report after one of his high school informants reported the rumor to him via text message.

Miss Cannon tapped on his door, and Mr. Ryland quickly shut his notebook and unlocked the door.

"Were you able to help Ms. Odom? She seemed pretty upset."

"Not really. We don't have all the facts on the case yet."

"Oh."

"Sometimes parents jump the gun too quickly and don't give us time to do a thorough investigation of the events."

"Is there anything that I can help with?"

"Yes, print out the schedules of DeCalia Thomas, Jessica Barnes, and Alexandra Kent and give them to me as soon as you can."

"Right away."

Mr. Ryland looked at his trophy case.

"Running a high school is harder than playing college ball and playing in the NBA combined," he said before sighing.

When Mr. Ryland was recruited to be the principal at Barry High, he was attractive because he was from the Maryland/DC area, he had a fan base from his Washington Bullets playing days, and he'd become somewhat of a businessman in the DC area, owning a couple of donut and coffee shops. But every day, as more violence crept into

Barry High, Mr. Ryland thought it was a total mistake for him to be there at all.

Chapter 7

Ahmed sat in the corner of the lunchroom. His eyes burned with anger because the rumors had circulated all morning that Calia, Jessica, and Alexandra jumped Tashera. All of the guys from the basketball team told him that it was messed up, but that didn't change the facts. He was the one who knew Jessica, and Tashera really had nothing to do with how Ahmed treated Jessica.

Ahmed dated Jessica last year and all throughout the summer. They met in geometry class. Jessica was a cute girl, brown-skinned and wore her reddish brown hair in a curly bob. When they first started dating, Jessica was always by herself at home and willing to do anything to get him over there. In the beginning, Ahmed liked how Jessica worshipped him, called him in the morning to wake him up, and stopped hanging out with her girls to be with him. But after about three months, it started to get really boring. He only kept dating her because he could have sex with her whenever he wanted. All the guys on the team knew Ahmed and Jessica were doing it because they'd caught them behind the bleachers after a practice. Ahmed remembered how it felt to get ribbed by the guys when they talked about him and Jessica.

"I saw the way Jessica was handlin' you earlier," Mike joked.

"What are you talking about?" Ahmed responded.

"Y'all was getting' busy behind the bleachers."

Ahmed stopped in his tracks. "You were there?"

"Yeah, you lucky I wasn't taping. She's a real freak. You got it good."

"I ain't even feelin' her like that. It's just something to do."

"Well a lot of us wish we had something to do like that."

"Whatever man."

"You really don't care about her?"

"Nah. Please, it ain't nuthin'"

"What if me and a couple of the guys wanted to tap that? Would you mind?"

"I just told you that I didn't care, didn't I?"

"You are like the coolest, Ahmed. Give me a pound."

Ahmed shook Mike's hand, not realizing that Jessica had told Mike she'd have sex with him if Ahmed was cool with it.

"So you gonna talk to her about it man?" Mike asked.

"I'll see what I can make happen," Ahmed replied.

As Ahmed left out a side door of the cafeteria, Jessica and her crew walked in with Jessica wearing dark clothing, bulky black work boots, black mascara over her eyelids, and dark brown lipstick.

****

Khalil lifted the dumbbells in his left hand twenty-five times and then repeated the same exercise with his right hand. When he was an active member of Deuce Trés, he performed 300 bicep curls per arm, per day. Last night when he returned from the hospital, he decided that he would call some of the girls down with Deuce Trés and get them to find out who attacked Tashera.

He picked up his phone and dialed Darren's old house number.

"Hello," the woman said on the other end.

"Lady B?" Khalil asked.

"Yeah. Who's this?"

"It's Khalil."

"Who?"

"Khalil-the lieutenant."

"Umph. I must be the last person on earth."

Khalil smoothed his beard. He remembered the times that Lady B would hang out with him, Darren, and the crew. She was what they called a down for whatever chick. She'd carry weapons in her waist and walk into the club. She was so pretty that she rarely got frisked or patted down like other women did and especially not like any of the men did. She was Darren's main girl and she was waiting for him to finish a ten-year bid so they could live happily ever after.

"You remember my baby sister, Tashera?"

"She had the long ponytail down in back, right?"

"Yeah. Well, yesterday she was jumped in Southeast by a group of girls wearing hoodies and she ain't even built like that. She's a square."

"That's a raw deal."

"I need you to find out who did it."

"I can't. I'm laying low."

Khalil paused. He knew that the entire crew treated him differently after they realized that he wouldn't be able to walk anymore. If Darren was still a soldier on the streets, B would have jumped to assist him.

"B, before I got in this wheelchair, I always had your back and Darren's. I never asked you for nothin'. You can't desert me. I'm a part of the family – even though you see me as a cripple."

"I'll put my ear down and get back to you."

"That's what's up, B. The sooner the better." Khalil rolled himself over to the bathroom. He didn't exactly know what he'd do once he found out who beat down his sister, but crippled or not, he was going to do something.

****

Detective Stewart printed out the vehicle registration information of the car that carried Tashera's attackers. It was registered to an Anita Thomas who lived in the Deuce Five area of Southeast. He called a female colleague, Detective Ericka Rodriguez, to his office.

"What's up Stew?" Detective Rodriguez asked.

"I'm heading over to Greater Southeast Community Hospital to interview an assault victim. Depending on what the victim remembers and my subsequent investigation, this case could be an atom bomb and blow up the issue of violence in the District."

"You need me to come and take pictures?"

"And if she prefers to talk to a woman instead of me, I may need you to be the lead."

"When are you leaving?"

"Now."

"Do you think this assault had gang ties?" Rodriguez asked.

"I'm not that far into the investigation yet, but it's possible."

Chapter 8

Tashera looked in the mirror. For the first time since her facial bandages were removed, she could see the scar that formed above her naturally arched eyebrows. She saw the split of her full bottom lip. Ahmed told her over and over again, "You have the best lips." *Bet he won't think so now,* she thought.

Ever since she started dating Ahmed, a lot of the girls in her school started acting differently toward her. The ones that used to say hello in the hallway stopped speaking unless they were her clients. And even some of her clients stopped coming to her to get their weaves sewed in after word spread through the school that she and Ahmed were an item. Tashera always tried to be cool with whoever was in school. She didn't care if they had a boyfriend or not. It didn't matter. If they treated her fairly, then she would treat them the same. But now, everything was different.

She pulled her notebook and a pen out of her book bag, and across the front of her notebook she wrote HATE in big, bold letters. She felt around in her book bag and pulled out *The Blueprint for My Girls*, a book by Yasmin Shiraz. The author had come to Marion Barry High School last month to talk to girls about life choices. Tashera flipped to page 21 and read the heading, "Be a person with good morals and solid values." She shook her head. *My good morals didn't get me anything but jumped,* she thought. Tashera put the book down as her mobile phone rang.

"Hello."

"Tashera, it's me Kiki. How are you?"

"Fine."

"I heard you were in the hospital."

"Yeah, some stuff went down yesterday."

"Girl, it's all over school."

"What are they saying?"

"That you got jumped because of Ahmed."

"What? Ahmed? What does he have to do with it?" Tashera asked.

"I heard that one of the six girls that jumped you, one of them is his girlfriend."

Tashera frowned as her anger grew. "That's a total lie."

"I'm just telling you what I heard."

"Yeah, whatever. So what's next?"

"I heard you had two broken arms. Is that true?"

"No Kiki. That ain't true either. But I gotta go. Bye."

Tashera hung up from Kiki and called Ahmed's phone, which went straight into voice mail. Tashera was angrier than two pit bulls fighting over a piece of meat.

"It's Tashera, your girlfriend or so I thought until a few minutes ago. Somebody just told me that I got jumped because of you. What is up with that, Ahmed? You better call me back as soon as you get this message."

Tashera attempted to lie on her side, but her ribs hurt too much. She put her head down on the pillow and cried quietly to herself.

****

Sheila walked into Tashera's room with the smell of fried fish wafting about her. The smell awakened Tashera from her sad dreams.

"How's my baby girl?" Sheila asked smiling wide as the Grand Canyon.

"Mom, you don't have to pretend you're happy. I know you're not."

"I just don't want to bring you down," Sheila said and opened a fish dinner for Tashera.

"I'm already beneath the ground. I'm waiting to see a pitchfork."

"I went to your school today."

"For what?"

"To see the principal. I wanted to know if he'd heard anything about the girls who attacked you."

"What did he say?"

"He said that he hadn't really heard anything, but he was lying."

"How do you know that, Mom?"

"You know I've always known when people are lying. It's just something that I know. And he was definitely lying."

"I wish this never happened."

"Me too. I will be getting to the bottom of it. Don't worry. I'll be like a Law & Order episode."

Tashera cracked a slight smile.

There was a tapping on Tashera's door. Sheila and Tashera both looked toward the door and saw a tall, thin black man and an average-sized Spanish woman looking back at them.

"Hello ladies. We're detectives Stewart and Rodriguez," Detective Stewart said. "We need to talk to you about what happened yesterday."

Sheila looked the two detectives up and down and said, "Come on in."

"I'm the head of the Gang Prevention Division…"

"Gang? What does this have to do with a gang?" Sheila asked.

"What's your name, ma'am?"

40

"My name is Sheila Odom. You can call me Sheila, and that's my daughter Tashera."

"Sheila, the area in which your daughter was attacked is a zone that's frequently been the site of gang-related scuffles. So, I have to ask is Tashera associated, involved, or affiliated in a gang in any way?"

Sheila sucked her teeth. "You must be kidding me. If you think this is her fault, you need to get out of here. She was attacked. She's practically a straight A student. Just because she cut through a parking lot that gangs fight on doesn't mean she's a member of the gang. Who'd you sleep with to get your job?"

Detective Rodriguez chuckled quietly.

"Ms. Odom, let me ask all the questions so that everything will be ruled out. I would hate to make assumptions and then those things bite us later. Can you understand that?"

"Barely," Sheila said and sucked her teeth again.

"Tashera, no matter how ridiculous the questions sound, just answer them to the best of your ability. I'm creating a file for this case. I want to make sure that we pursue and catch whoever did this to you. So, I need your full cooperation. Do you understand?"

"Yes."

After asking Tashera to spell her name and state her age, Detective Stewart asked, "What happened to you yesterday?"

"I went to school. I was hungry at the end of the day, so I decided to go to the mini-mart close to my house."

"Which school do you attend and what's the name of the mini-mart?"

"Marion Barry Senior High and Meha's Mini Mart."

"Okay, go ahead."

"I bought some snacks for me and my brother."

"Was your brother with you? How old is he and what's his name?"

"My brother is twenty-two. His name is Khalil. He looks forward to seeing me after school. Anyway, I'm walking home eating my oatmeal crème pie and three girls surround me when I'm in the parking lot."

"Did you know these girls?"

"No."

"What did they look like?"

"They had on dark hoodies with dark glasses. One was short, one was skinny, and one was big-boned. They were all black, though the short one was light-skinned."

"Do you know why this happened? Were you getting threatened by anyone at school?"

Tashera looked out the window.

"I don't know why I got jumped, but I started getting notes in my locker about three weeks ago."

"What kind of notes?"

"Notes that said," she paused before adding, 'Stay away from Ahmed.'"

"Who is Ahmed?"

"He's my boyfriend."

"Why didn't you tell me people were threatening you?" Sheila interjected.

"I didn't want to worry you. Ever since I started dating Ahmed, a lot of the girls in school don't even talk to me anymore."

"Are you sure he don't have a bunch of girls on the side and they're jealous of you?" Sheila asked. "Maybe this is why all this stuff has gone down. It's probably his fault."

"Let's not jump to conclusions, Ms. Odom," Detective Stewart said. "Can you give me a number for Ahmed?"

"Sure," Tashera said, slightly shrugging.

Tashera ripped out a page of her notebook and gave it to the detective.

"Ms. Odom and Tashera, we need to take pictures of Tashera's bruises to put in the file. My partner, Detective Rodriguez would take them while I step out of the room. Is that okay?"

"It's fine with me," Tashera said. Sheila just nodded. Within five minutes, all of the pictures had been taken and Sheila decided to step out of the room to talk with Detective Stewart.

****

Detective Stewart read over his notes as Sheila approached him.

"Have you visited her school yet?" she asked.

"Not yet."

"Well I have."

"What happened?"

"I know every mother thinks that her child is a good kid, but my daughter actually is. I don't think she's ever gotten into one fistfight in her entire life. She's been the type of kid to keep a low profile and generally people like her. She isn't flashy; she doesn't really talk about people. She just comes home, and she does hair. That's it. So, I'm very mad about this situation. I went to her principal to find out if he looked into the situation."

"And what did he say?"

"He lied. He told me that he didn't really know anything. I'm not a detective, but I know when people are lying. He knows something, and he didn't tell me. I don't know if he has information that can help my daughter's case or if he has information to protect the attackers. I really don't know. "

"Thank you for that information."

"I hope you use it and get to the bottom of this mess before I do. 'Cause in the event that I'm faster than you are, nobody in the district is gonna like what I do."

"Are you telling me I need to put you under surveillance?"

"I'm telling you that a bunch of no good little wenches hurt my only daughter, and I'm not gonna sit back and let them go unpunished. That's truly what I'm saying."

Sheila went back into Tashera's hospital room as Detective Rodriguez was coming out.

"It looks like we need to make a trip to Barry High, too," Detective Stewart said. "I'm a little worried. The mother is moving faster than we are."

"Is she conducting her own investigation?" Detective Rodriguez asked.

"It definitely sounds like it."

Chapter 9

Ahmed listened to Tashera's voicemail the minute he finished with basketball practice. He knew he had to tell her about the rumors and Jessica, but he really didn't want to because he knew it could ruin his relationship with Tashera.

Ahmed recalled his relationship with Jessica last summer. It was bad enough he had treated Jessica like a piece of meat, but letting his boys tap her, too, went way over the line of decency.

He had told Mike that he'd handle things with Jessica, and he wasted no time doing so. Later that day, after talking to Mike, Ahmed told Jessica he was coming to visit her. He told her that he wanted to wrap a scarf around her eyes so she couldn't see what he was doing. Once he wrapped her eyes, he went downstairs and led Mike into her bedroom. Mike started to have sex with her though Jessica thought it was Ahmed, that is, until she took off the scarf.

"Ahmed, what is going on?" Jessica yelled.

Ahmed came into the bedroom. "I didn't think you'd really have sex with him, so I just helped it along. It's like a favor for me. So thanks."

Ahmed passed Jessica around to his friends like a dinner platter and had the nerve to dump her, telling her, "I can't be with a girl who sleeps with my best friend and all of my teammates. I need a girl who thinks for herself. You're too much of a follower."

But Jessica told him that he'd regret the day he ever met her. Now that Tashera had been jumped and Jessica was

45

to blame, Ahmed definitely regretted having treated Jessica so badly.

****

Ahmed brought a teddy bear to Tashera's hospital room. Tashera's mom was lying at the foot of her bed when he walked in.

"Hello," Ahmed said.

"Who are you?" Sheila asked.

"I'm Ahmed."

Tashera turned her head and looked out the window.

"I brought a li'l something for you, Shera."

Ahmed pushed the teddy bear in Tashera's direction but she didn't respond.

"I really need to talk to you. This situation isn't my fault, but I'll do everything I can to explain it to you and resolve it."

"What situation?" Sheila asked.

Tashera looked at her mother.

"Mom, I need to speak to Ahmed in private. Could you go to the cafeteria and get me some fries or something?"

"I want to hear about this situation, too. Why you kickin' me to the curb like I'm Homer Simpson?"

"Mom, please."

Sheila walked out the room and Ahmed walked over to Tashera and kissed her on the forehead.

"Don't come all up in my spot being all lovey-dovey and kissey when you're the reason that I'm in here in the first place. Who is the skank that you're still going with behind my back?" Tashera sat up in the bed. Her ribs hurt, but she sat as upright as she could.

"It's nothing like that. Tashera, calm down."

"Don't tell me to calm down. Tell me the truth."

"Everybody at school is saying that the girl Jessica that I used to mess with is behind all of this. I dated her last year and in the summer, but I broke it off before I even met you."

"I don't believe you," Tashera stated with her arms folded across her chest.

"What can I do to prove to you that I'm telling the truth?"

"Call her on the phone right now and tell her that you want to see her."

"For what?"

"I want to be there and see how she reacts. I'll know if you're telling the truth then."

"You can't leave the hospital yet."

"They'll be releasing me in a few days."

"The girl Jessica, she's mental. After we'd been kickin' it for a while, one of my friends wanted to have sex with her because I didn't really care for her that much. I told her to do it. Then I told her to have sex with a lot of guys on the team."

"Why would you do that?" Tashera screamed.

"It made me even more popular on the team. One of the guys bought me a new pair of Jordan's. Another person got me a Gilbert Arenas jersey. At first I did it because I didn't care and then I did it because the guys were hooking me up. It was like Christmas."

"That's so stupid. I like have no respect for you right now."

"She didn't have to do it. She was stupid. You wouldn't do anything like that if I asked you to do it."

"You got that right because I know how weak-minded boys are."

"After I stopped talking to Jessica, after she slept with everybody, she said that she hated me and that I was going to pay for what I'd done to her."

Tashera just shook her head.

"Jumping me? That's her way to pay you back. I'm a freaking innocent bystander. I'm attacked by some turtle that you turned out. Get out of my room. I can't talk to you anymore. You're too stupid for me."

"Tashera, I love you."

"Save it. If this is love, hate me. Just hate me."

Ahmed left Tashera's room as quickly as he'd entered, the only thing on his mind – making Jessica pay for hurting Tashera, the only girl he'd ever truly loved.

****

Khalil rolled himself into Tashera's hospital room and heard her crying. It was a sound he never got used to. He gently stroked her arm.

"Why are you crying?" Khalil asked.

"It's nothing."

"It's something or you wouldn't be crying."

Tashera didn't want to tell Khalil. Over the years, she saw how Khalil could never control his anger. When she was seven years old, Khalil made the next-door neighbor carry his books for a week because he'd accidentally bumped into Khalil and knocked his backpack off of his shoulder. Khalil screamed at their neighbor for fifteen straight minutes.

But now, she needed someone to share everything that Ahmed had just told her.

"My boyfriend just told me some girl he used to mess with is the person who jumped me."

"What?"

"Yeah, this girl that he dated a while ago. She's mental or something. She was trying to get back at him and so she and her friends jumped me. And I had nothing to do with how he even treated her last year. I wasn't even there!"

Tashera cried uncontrollably while Khalil's eyes reddened.

"Do you know if the girls were down with Deuce Five?" he asked.

"Come on, Khalil. I don't know that. Don't start with me. You think everything is about you and the Deuce Trés and the Deuce Five. This is about a bunch of jealous winches!"

"Anything involving you will always be gang affiliated because you're my li'l sister. That's just the way it is."

"I didn't ask you to be a part of a gang."

"No, but how you think you got through school all these years without no girls ever trying you or stepping to you at all? You think it's your winning personality? It's not."

Tashera stopped crying.

"Nobody messed with you because they knew you were protected. You were Deuce Trés protected. And now those girls have violated the protection."

"You are an ego-maniac! You never give me credit for anything."

Khalil backed up his wheelchair. He was tired of arguing with Tashera. She'd never accept that his gang ties prevented her from even having arguments with neighborhood girls. In their neighborhood, you could barely survive if you didn't have some kind of protection.

"What was the girl's name that was responsible? Did your boyfriend tell you that?"

"I'm not telling you. I can handle this on my own."

"I know you can, but you won't. I won't let you."

"Khalil, I can handle my own battles. I don't want Deuce Trés getting involved in this."

"I'm sorry babygirl, Deuce Trés was involved the moment one of the girls stopped you on your way home. This is the gang's fight now."

Sheila walked in and saw Tashera's swollen eyes.
"Are you okay, Tashera?"

"Yeah, I'm just tired," she said before lightly turning over and lying down. "I'll see you guys tomorrow. I just want to rest."

Sheila grabbed the two handles on Khalil's wheelchair and they left the hospital.

Chapter 10

Detectives Stewart and Rodriguez pulled onto 17th Street in SE. Detective Stewart looked at the vehicle registration information again.

"This is it. 3325 17th Street. We're looking for Anita Thomas."

"Got it," Detective Rodriguez said and ran her fingers along the top of her sidearm.

The detective approached the front porch and heard loud rap music filtering from inside the house. Detective Stewart knocked. There was no response, so he knocked again. A lady who looked to be in her early thirties opened the door. Detective Stewart flashed his badge.

"I'm Detective Stewart. This is my partner Detective Rodriguez. We're looking for Anita Thomas."

"I'm Anita. What did little Tommy do now?"

"Who?" Detective Stewart asked.

"My son. Y'all cops are always coming to my door telling me about something else you think he's done. So what did he do?"

"Oh. We have nothing to report on Tommy at this time, but where were you yesterday between one and five in the afternoon?"

"A lot of places."

"Can you be more specific?"

Anita dug in her shirt pocket and took out a pack of cigarettes. She lit one.

"At one o'clock, I was here in the house sleeping. At two o'clock, I was on my way to work, and from three to eleven-thirty, I was on my job."

"Where do you work?"

"LadyPower."

"You have a number so I can verify this information?"

"Yeah."

"Anita, who else lives here besides you and Tommy?"

"My daughter DeCalia and my cousin Fran."

"How did you get to work yesterday?"

"I rode the metro."

"Do you have a car?"

"What kind of question of that. Just because I ride the metro, you think that means I can't afford a car. You're unbelievable. Stop wasting my time." Anita reached toward the door panel to shut the door, but Detective Stewart raised his hand.

"Ma'am these questions are part of an investigation. I'd appreciate your assistance."

Anita took a long drag of her cigarette.

"Where's your car?" Detective Rodriguez asked.

"It's a couple of cars ahead. It's parked by the stop sign."

"Would you mind showing it to us?"

Anita looked down at her black bedroom slippers. She'd walked to the metro in her slippers, so she could surely walk a couple of paces to point to her car.

"Come on," she said.

Anita led the detectives to her car and said, "Here it is, my own Chevy Oldsmobile. It's old, but it was a gift from my father."

"Did you drive it yesterday?" Detective Stewart asked.

"No."

"Do you ever let anyone else drive it?"

"No."

"Ever?"

"Nobody else in the house has a driver's license. So what's the point?"

"Have you ever reported your car stolen?" Detective Rodriguez asked.

"No."

"To your knowledge has it ever been stolen?"

Anita rolled her eyes. "I don't think so. If somebody stole it, they would have never brought it back, right?"

"Right, for the most part. How old is your daughter?"

"Sixteen."

"What school does she go to?"

"Marion Barry High."

"What do she and Tommy do when you're at work in the evenings?"

"They stay at home with Fran, or they go hang out with friends."

"What's Fran's last name?"

"Sellers."

"Is Fran here now?"

"No, she went out of town."

"When?"

"Three days ago."

"Well, we'll need to talk to her. Do you know when she'll be back?"

"Any day now."

"Well, thank you for your time. Give Miss Sellers this business card and tell her to call me when she gets back in town."

Anita took the card from Detective Stewart as if it was diseased. She went back into her house and closed the door.

Detectives Stewart and Rodriguez sat back in the car and let the silence envelop them for a moment.

"It looks like her kids weren't supervised during the time of the attack," Detective Stewart said, "so one of them could have been the driver, but easily both of them could have been there. Tomorrow, let's visit the high school."

Detective Rodriguez nodded.

Chapter ii

Wednesday, April 4
Two days after the attack

Jessica, Calia, and Alexandra huddled in the girls' bathroom before first period.

"I got a note to report to the principal's office," Alexandria said, a light-skinned, small-framed girl who wore denim jeans and a white shirt with blue lettering that said YOU KNOW YOU WANT ME. "My teacher just gave it to me." She bit the nails on her left hand.

"What do you think it's for?" Jessica asked.

"I don't know," Alexandra replied. "But what if it has to do with that stuff that went down?"

"We all had on hoodies and glasses. Nobody saw us, so there's no way we'll get caught," Calia said.

"Yesterday I heard that Tashera's brother is like the top kid in the Deuce Trés gang. Did y'all hear that?"

Alexandra started pacing.

"I bet Ahmed is sad now. His little Miss Perfect being in the hospital and all," Jessica said. "The principal could be calling you down there to join the homecoming decorating committee or something. Don't panic. Nobody saw us. We're in the clear."

"If nobody saw us, why is there so much whispering every time I walk by in the hallway?" Alexandra asked.

"Because stupid, I wanted a couple of people to tell Ahmed what happened so he'd feel like the loser that he is."

Alexandra shook her head and started biting the nails on her other hand. The bell rang and she watched Calia and Jessica head to their first period classes. She headed straight to the principal's office.

****

Mr. Ryland looked over his notes on Alexandra Kent. She was a junior, a B/C student but hadn't been in any real trouble since entering Barry High. Both of her parents lived in the home and she was an only child. Last year she started hanging with DeCalia Thomas and some of her teachers noted that her grades went from A/B to B/C. That wasn't a terribly high price to pay for a new friendship, if that's all the influence that DeCalia had over Alexandra. Yesterday after school, Mr. Ryland had interrogated his high school informant about the personalities of Alexandra, DeCalia, and Jessica.

"What are these girls like?" he asked. "None of them have even been suspended before except DeCalia. If they committed this attack, what drives them?"

"DeCalia is the leader," Moab, his informant, replied. "She has always been a bully. She's gotten into fights over the smallest things. She just likes to fight."

"Why would a girl like Alexandra be friends with a bully?"

"Alexandra wants to fit in. She wants to be cool. She doesn't want to be bullied by anybody. So, when she started being friends with DeCalia, it solved a lot of her problems. She has a bully as a friend, so nobody will bother with her."

Mr. Ryland thought about the rationale. It was the same thought-process that led so many boys to try-out for high school sports. They wanted to be perceived as athletic, thereby untouchable in many cases. Bullies in schools rarely hassled the athletes.

"What's Jessica's story?"

"She's a head case," Moab said.

"What do you mean?"

"As a sophomore, she was best-dressed, popular always had the baddest hairstyles and she was Ahmed- the basketball player's girlfriend. I don't know what happened over the summer, but when she came back to school, she was wearing black every day, her hair was in a ponytail or under some kind of scully. She wears black eyeliner or mascara smeared across her eyelids. She looks like a devil worshipper most days."

"What do you think her role would be in this attack against Tashera?"

"I don't know, but since Jessica used to date Ahmed and now Tashera does, it was probably her idea."

Mr. Ryland's door opened and Alexandra Kent entered.

"Sit down, Miss Kent." As soon as Alexandra's bottom touched the seat, Mr. Ryland asked, "Where were you Monday, April 2nd after school?"

"Home."

"Was anybody home with you?"

"No."

Alexandra started twirling the end of her ponytail.

"Do you know Tashera Odom?"

"No."

"You don't know anything about her?"

"No."

"A group of girls jumped her on Monday."

"She should be more careful," Alexandra said.

"Really. Are you careful?"

"Yes."

"Is there anything you want to tell me about what you were doing on Monday?"

"I wasn't doing anything. Watching TV, reading a book. Besides that, no."

"Get a note to return to class from Miss Cannon. You're dismissed."

Mr. Ryland had only begun conducting interviews of high school students and getting them to confess wasn't his strong suit. Maybe instead of pretending to know what he was doing, he should call someone in law enforcement to help in sorting out the mess.

"Miss Cannon, come here please. I'm thinking about inviting the police to interview the three girls who I suspect are behind the attack on Tashera Odom."

"I don't know about that, Mr. Ryland. The school board gets jumpy when the police get involved."

"If none of those girls confesses, there needs to be an investigation, and no one here knows the first thing about conducting one. We need to partner with somebody who does."

"I'm just telling you it's not going to be the popular decision."

"What? Trying to find out who attacked a high school student as quickly as possible? That's not going to be popular? Why not?"

"That's not how they do things here, and I've been in the school system for ten years. When outsiders are invited to help us, it sends out the message that the school is incompetent and can't do their job."

"I need to think for a few moments, Miss Cannon."

"Sure."

Miss Cannon shut his office door.

"What have I gotten myself into?" Mr. Ryland asked himself out loud.

****

Since Tashera's attack, Khalil had made himself more visible in the street. He reconnected with his boy Fitz, and he started frequenting his old haunts. Around lunchtime Khalil sat at the edge of Marion Barry High School's property. He waited for a Deuce Trés soldier to come out and give him pictures of the three girls who were responsible for the attack on Tashera. The junior soldier had already told Khalil that the attack was out of jealousy and had nothing to do with the rival crew Deuce Five. For Khalil, it didn't matter why they did it. The three girls would be given punishment according to what they had done and who they had done it to.

Before long, two Deuce Trés high school soldiers spotted Khalil near the fence. They handed Khalil three pictures-one each of Alexandra, DeCalia, and Jessica.

"Good work," Khalil said and shook hands with both ninth grade boys.

"If you need us to smoke 'em, let us know," one of the boys said.

"I got it from here. But keep your ears to the ground for me."

"Peace Soldier."

"Peace."

The Deuce Trés soldiers always ended their meetings wishing each other peace though in their hearts they knew they were about to wreak havoc and violence.

Khalil put the photos in his jacket pocket and then dialed his cell phone.

"I need to meet with two of your girls."

"Sure, when?" Lady B asked.

"Tomorrow would be good. It's time for the payback."

"We'll meet you at the old spot around dinner time."

"Peace," Khalil said and hung up.

Chapter 12

Thursday, April 5
Three days after the attack

Sheila Odom went into Khalil's bedroom before she headed off to work. She saw a picture of a girl on the floor.

"I didn't know he was trying to have a girlfriend," Sheila mumbled.

Sheila picked up the photo and turned it over. The back of the photo read: CALIA THOMAS. 3325 17TH STREET. Sheila dropped the photo.

Calia is the girl who attacked Tashera, she thought. She went back into her room and changed into a black sweat suit and black Timberland boots. She took off all of her jewelry. She ran outside and cranked up her car. She was headed to the home of Calia Thomas.

****

Detectives Stewart and Rodriguez parked on a side street adjacent to Marion Barry High School.

"Do you think the principal is going to cooperate with us?" Detective Rodriguez asked.

"If we emphasize that kids' lives are in danger, hopefully, he'll see the light."

"Here's to hoping." Detective Rodriguez raised her Styrofoam cup of coffee and took one last swig.

The detectives passed through metal detectors that went off when they entered, but there were no guards standing watch, so they were able to proceed directly to the principal's office. After they flashed their badges to Miss Cannon, they were ushered into Mr. Ryland's office.

"Sean Ryland, it's a pleasure to meet you," Mr. Ryland said and extended his hand.

"I'd forgotten how tall you were," Detective Stewart said as he craned his neck upward.

"Have we met before?"

"No, but I was and am a big Washington Bullets fan. I followed your playing days."

"I appreciate that. What brings you to my school today?"

"We want to know what you know about the attack on Tashera Odom."

Mr. Ryland sat down.

"In that case, I'm glad you're here."

Mr. Ryland explained everything he had learned about Alexandra, DeCalia, and Jessica through his informant.

"I've already interviewed Alexandra Kent even though it didn't go that well," he said. "What I'd like you to do is interview DeCalia Thomas. I can set you up in a conference room around the corner. I'll sit in and we can get to the bottom of this. Technically, I'm able to talk to the kids without parent's permission, though the police aren't. So technically I'll be doing the interview, but help me as I go along."

"Got it," Detective Stewart said. "What do you know about DeCalia Thomas?"

"She's been suspended several times for fighting, inciting riots, taunting, those kinds of things."

"Recently?"

"No, actually before I got here. But she's a junior, and all through ninth and tenth grades she was constantly in trouble. As a matter of fact, she got held back the first time she tried ninth grade."

"I'll get Miss Cannon to show you to the conference room, and we'll get DeCalia Thomas down here right away."

Detectives Stewart and Rodriguez followed Miss Cannon down a hallway into a room on the left.

After Miss Cannon left the room, Detective Stewart sat down.

"Is it me or do I detect some cooperation from the head of this school?" he asked, sarcastically.

"Yeah. He seemed really relieved that 5-0 walked through the door."

"No kidding."

Within a few minutes, DeCalia Thomas was brought into the conference room.

"Miss Thomas, this is Detective Stewart and Detective Rodriguez," Mr. Ryland said, bringing up the rear. "I've asked them to help me because I have some troubling concerns that I need to speak with you about."

DeCalia looked at the detectives and turned her lips upward.

"Have a seat," Detective Stewart said.

As DeCalia walked to the chair at the furthest side of the table, Detective Stewart looked at her shoes and noticed some red spots. *That could be blood*, he thought. *She's one brazen young lady.*

"Let's cut to the chase, did you attack Tashera Odom on Monday, April 2nd?" Mr. Ryland asked.

"Who?"

"Tashera Odom."

"I don't know who you're talking about."

Detective Stewart cut in, "Miss Thomas, where did you go after school on Monday?"

"I went home."

"How did you get home?"

"I walked."

"Were you by yourself?"

"No. I had my girl Alexandra with me."

Mr. Ryland added, "That's strange because when I spoke with Alexandra, she said she wasn't with you. She said she was home by herself on Monday."

"Oh, oh, right. I got that mixed up with yesterday. I went home by myself, too."

"Was anyone there when you got home who can verify that you were there?" Detective Stewart asked.

"Yeah, my cousin Fran."

Detective Stewart scribbled on his notepad. DeCalia's mother told him that Fran was out of town on Monday, April 2nd.

"Do you remember what you wore to school on Monday?"

"Yeah, some jeans, a sweatshirt, and some boots."

DeCalia looked down. "These boots probably."

Detective Stewart signaled to Detective Rodriguez that they needed to leave the room.

"Mr. Ryland, please continue. We'll be right back in a few minutes."

As soon as he closed the door behind them, Detective Stewart turned to Rodriguez and said, "We already know her family's car was spotted at the scene, and it looks like she has blood on her boot right now. The boot is in plain sight. We can definitely arrest her under the suspicion of aggravated assault. We'll send her boot to the lab for analysis immediately. It'll probably be a perfect match to Tashera's DNA."

"I'll call for back-up," Detective Rodriguez said.

"Good. I'm going to keep asking her questions until the uniforms get here."

Detective Stewart stepped back into the room.

"Do you know how to drive, DeCalia?" Detective Stewart asked.

"A little."

"You don't have your license yet?"

"No."

"Do you have a learner's permit?"

"Yeah."

"Did you hang out with Jessica Barnes on Monday?" Mr. Ryland asked.

"No."

"She told me that she was with you."

"What difference does it make? All of these days run together. We're all friends. Sometimes we hang out, other times we don't. Maybe we were together on Monday. Maybe it was Tuesday. I can't remember all these days."

"Did you tell your mom that you took her car on Monday?" Detective Stewart asked.

"No."

"Where did you take her car on Monday?"

"I just rode up to the fish joint and back home."

A few minutes later, Detective Rodriguez tapped on the door with two policemen in uniform standing behind her. Detective Stewart stood.

"What is going on?" DeCalia asked as one of the uniform policemen put her hands behind her back.

Detective Stewart mirandized DeCalia. "Do you understand these rights that have been read to you?" he asked.

"Since she's a minor and her parents are not present, I will ride with her and stay in the police station until her parents come or an attorney," Mr. Ryland said.

"That's fine," Detective Stewart said and walked out of the conference room, pulling DeCalia by her elbow.

"You can't do this. I'm going to sue y'all. You ain't supposed to talk to me without my parents here," DeCalia said.

"After we book you, we'll find exactly where your parents are," Detective Rodriguez said.

As they walked out the front of the school, students stood in the hallway and watched DeCalia be escorted out in handcuffs.

****

Sheila's heart raced as she parked in front of Calia Thomas' house. She put her cell phone deep into her pocket and stepped out of the car. She trotted up the cracked walkway and knocked on the old blue door. No one responded. Sheila knocked again and heard some movement from the inside of the house.

"Open this door or I'm gonna knock it down," Sheila said as she readied her foot to kick the bottom of the door.

Anita opened the door with a baseball bat in her hand.

"Who are you knocking on my door like you crazy?" she said.

"I'm looking for Calia Thomas. Is she here?"

"No, she ain't here."

"I don't believe you." Sheila, taller than Anita Thomas, brushed passed her. "Calia!"

"I'm going to give you three seconds to get out of my house or explain what you're doing, or I'm going to crack your head open with my bat."

Sheila turned around. "Are you Calia's mom?"

"What of it?"

"Well on Monday, your daughter and two of her friends jumped my daughter for no reason. I came here to whup her butt 'cause obviously you ain't done enough of that with her."

Anita drew the bat back and swung it toward Sheila's head. Sheila ducked and punched Anita in the jaw and in the abdomen. Anita dropped the bat and lunged toward Sheila, knocking her back onto a glass table that shattered with the weight of the two women. Sheila attempted to push herself up with her left and stabled it in an array of shattered glass.

"Aww," Sheila said and pushed Anita off of her. Sheila grabbed Anita by the head and dragged her out of the house and proceeded to kick her on the front lawn.

"If you," Sheila kicked Anita in the back, "Or your daughter," Sheila kicked Anita in the leg, "ever come near my daughter again," Sheila kicked Anita in the chest, "I'll kill you, both of you." Then Sheila spit in Anita's face. Sheila turned and began to walk away from Anita, but Anita got up and wrestled her to the ground. Sirens were heard in the distance, a distance that grew shorter. Two policemen arrived as Sheila and Anita continued rolling on the ground and punching each other.

The officers jumped out of their cars and each policeman grabbed a woman and pulled her in the opposite direction of the other. Another police car pulled up. It was Detective Rodriguez and Detective Stewart. They saw Sheila Odom and Anita Thomas being handcuffed.

"I'll take her with me," Detective Stewart said and put Anita Thomas in his police car.

As he got back into the car and drove off, Stewart thought, *Now, I have to explain why mother and daughter will be sharing a jail cell today.*

Chapter 13

Ahmed had been calling Tashera since he woke up, but she wouldn't pick up her cell phone. He knew that she was disappointed in him and knowing that made him all the more angry with Jessica for turning his world upside down.

He reached for his cell phone and dialed.

"Hello," a female voice said.

"Jessica," Ahmed said, "I need to see you."

"For what?"

"I want to talk to you."

"Oh, now that your girl ain't hot no more, you want me back, is that it? I don't think so. I don't want to be your sloppy seconds."

"It's not that. I need to apologize to your face," Ahmed said and couldn't believe he'd said it. He didn't plan on apologizing to Jessica. When he saw her, he planned on making her confess on tape to what she did and then taking it to the police so that Tashera could file a complaint against her.

Tashera would have to forgive me if I could get a real confession from Jessica, he thought.

****

Khalil sat at a table at Downtown's Fish Shack and waited for Lady B to arrive. After a few moments passed, Lady B walked into the restaurant alone and in full couture.

"I thought I told you to bring two girls," Khalil said.

"Chill out. They're out back. Give me the details."

67

"I need your girls to snatch the girl in this picture tonight. I have an abandoned building that I want her to be brought back to. Her address is on the back of this picture."

Lady B looked at the picture. The girl looked like she could have been twelve years old if it weren't for all the raccoon make-up around her eyes.

"Have someone call me when it's done," Khalil added, "and I'll let them know where to meet me."

Lady B got up and said, "Peace."

"Peace," Khalil said before he ordered a fish sandwich with fries. Khalil wanted to go back to the hospital to visit Tashera, but he knew she'd still be angry about their argument over Deuce Trés. Tashera didn't get angry often, but when she did she held a grudge like a polar bear gripping a seal's head.

****

Tashera was wheeled down to the x-ray room. Her doctor had told her that after three days, he wanted to see how her ribs were healing.

"How are you feeling, Miss Odom?" the nurse asked her.

"I'm not as sore as I was yesterday, that's for sure."

Tashera was put in a full body x-ray machine and lights went off and on around her. Tashera closed her eyes and remembered the last time that she was in the hospital. She was four years old and had fallen off her bike. Her dad had been teaching her how to ride her bike without training wheels, but Tashera lost her balance and fell on the side of her head.

"Shee, Shee are you okay?"

Tashera looked up at her father whose eyes told her that she was in some kind of trouble so she started crying.

"My head hurts."

Ray looked at the side of his daughter's head and noticed that she had blood seeping from an open wound. He lifted Tashera from the ground, dragged her bicycle inside, and made a cold compress out of a rag wrapped around a couple pieces of ice.

"We're going to the hospital," Ray said. "I want the doctor to check you out."

"Yippee," Tashera said, "I'm riding in the ambulance!"

"Uh, no. Daddy's gonna drive you to the hospital."

Ray reached into his pocket and gave Tashera the lollipop that he'd been saving for her first day of riding her bike without her training wheels.

"Here baby. This is for trying as hard as you could out there."

Tashera ripped the candy wrapper off the lollipop.

"Thanks Daddy."

Tashera missed her father badly, especially at times like this. He would have known what to say to Khalil about getting his gang involved in Tashera's battles. Tashera knew that if her father were still alive, Khalil would never have even joined a gang. Her father was strong, a real leader. He died of a heart attack when Tashera was seven and Khalil was thirteen. It was the same year Khalil first started getting involved with Deuce Trés.

The nurse pulled Tashera out of the body x-ray machine.

"Do you need anything today?" the nurse asked.

"I could really use somebody to talk to," Tashera said.

Back in her room, Tashera flipped through various channels on the television. There was absolutely nothing on, as usual. She took *The Blueprint for My Girls* off her nightstand. She read a few pages and then stopped on page 83, where it read, "Family members aren't always your best advisers." *That's the understatement of the year*, Tashera thought. She took out her pad and pen and decided to write a letter to the book's author.

Miss Yasmin,

I don't know who else to go to with my problems. Nobody really understands. My mom doesn't understand, and my brother can't even hear me. He's not deaf, he just acts like it. My brother wants his crew to beat up the girls who attacked me. He's a member of a gang, and he doesn't appreciate me getting into a scuffle. I understand his point of view, but he can't always fight my battles. And anyway, the gang has nothing to do with it. I almost lost my brother four years ago when he was shot while doing some stuff with his "crew." My mother and I thought he was going to die. God spared him, but left him in a wheelchair. My brother doesn't understand that every time he talks about violence, I'm worried that he won't ever come home. I'm not as worried about me as I am about him. He doesn't get that.

You don't talk about violence much in your book, but violence is all around my family. It's tearing us apart because *everybody has their side and nobody wants to listen to mine.*

Your girl,
Tashera

Tashera yawned and closed her notebook. As her eyelids began to droop, she remembered that she wanted to call her mother at lunchtime. Her mother had gone back to work, and Tashera really wanted to talk to her about what to do about Ahmed.

Chapter 14

Detective Stewart sat in his office with Anita Thomas across from him. Anita looked like she'd been in a ten-vehicle pile up with her busted lip, two black eyes, lump on the side of her head, and all the other injuries you couldn't see, but could tell she had from the pained expression on her face.

"You weren't expecting to see me so soon were you?" Detective Stewart asked.

"No. Did you know all this was going down when you came to my house yesterday?" Anita asked.

"Not exactly. DeCalia admitted to taking your car, and it had been seen in the vicinity of the attack on Tashera Odom. Right now, we need you to convince DeCalia to cooperate with us."

"What for? So y'all can throw her under the jail? I didn't raise no rat."

"Ms. Thomas, the lady who attacked you- her daughter is in the hospital right now with broken ribs and all sorts of other injuries. As far as we can see, she was attacked without any provocation."

"And?"

"This means that your daughter is looking at ten to twenty years in prison for assault with intent to commit mayhem and aggravated assault. But, she didn't act alone. If she'd give up the other two girls, I'd let the district attorney know. I'd be in a better position to help her. The way it stands right now, she's going down."

"If that's all you gotta say, take me to my cell."

"Have it your way, Ms. Thomas. It seems you don't care as much about your daughter as I thought you did. What mother in her right mind would ignore their daughter potentially being sentenced for twenty years in prison? Does DeCalia know that you don't give a crap about her? Maybe that's why she's here in the first place."

"Whatever," Anita said and stood. "I didn't see you coming around helping when I was raising her, so you can't judge me."

Detective Stewart called for the uniformed policeman to take Anita Thomas to her cell.

He groaned. He knew that what Calia did was wrong, but he wasn't sure how he felt about her paying for that mistake with her life. If her mother wasn't going to help her, then he'd have to find a way to get through to DeCalia himself.

****

When Tashera awakened, she was surprised to find that three hours had passed and that her mother had not visited or called her. Tashera immediately called her mom's work phone that went into voicemail. Then Tashera dialed her cell phone that also went into voicemail. Tashera decided to call another lady at her mom's job-someone that she reached out to when she thought her mom was at a meeting at work.

"Mrs. Pendleton?"

"Yes."

"Hello there. It's Tashera, Sheila's daughter."

"How are you, baby? You're mom said there was a family emergency. Are you okay?" Mrs. Pendleton asked.

"I'm fine. Have you seen my mother today?"

"No, she was supposed to come in, but she never made it. We thought something came up with you."

"That's strange. I'll see if something happened with my brother."

Tashera called her brother's cell phone, and he didn't answer.

"What is going on with my family today?" Tashera asked out loud.

****

Sheila Odom stood in the corner of the holding cell in the 7th District police station. She'd been thrown into the cell after her altercation with DeCalia's mom. She looked down at her pants and noticed that the left leg of her sweat pant was torn. She looked around the cell. There were eleven other detainees in the cell. She looked over at a clock that was hanging outside the cell. It was already early evening and she hadn't talked to Tashera or Khalil all day.

I need to be there for my daughter, she thought. She looked around the cell again. *I can't help my daughter from here.*

"Guard, guard," Sheila yelled. A female guard approached the cell.

"Don't I get a phone call or something? I need to call my lawyer."

"Just a minute," the guard said and walked away.

"This is ridiculous," Sheila said.

"If you don't calm down, they're not going to let you use the phone at all," a lady in a gray pinstriped suit said.

"Mind your business."

The lady stared at the floor and shook her head.

The guard returned and said, "Odom?"

Sheila walked up to the bars.

"Yeah, I'm Sheila Odom."

"Detective Stewart needs to talk to you before your phone call. It's gonna be a while."

"Detective Stewart? I want to talk to his boss. He can't stop me from making a phone call."

The guard walked away.

"This must be her first time in here," a lady said dressed head to toe in plastic—plastic bra-top, skirt, and shoes. She looked at Sheila and chuckled.

"No kidding," the pinstriped lady said and laughed. "You don't get much accomplished by yelling at the guards." Sheila looked at the ladies laughing at her. She moved as far away from them as she could.

A woman who looked to be about nineteen walked over to Sheila.

"What's up, sista? My name is Nadia," she said.

"I ain't your sista."

"I was just tryin' to make polite conversation."

"Oh. Go 'head," Sheila said.

"What you in for?"

"Fightin'."

"An old broad like you?" Nadia asked.

"Who you callin' a broad?"

"I meant no disrespect, but I didn't think women your age got into scuffles."

"Somebody put their hands on my daughter, so I had to do what I had to do."

"No doubt. Where's your daughter now?"

"In the hospital."

"Does she know where you are?"

Sheila didn't respond. Tashera would be worried about her, she thought.

"I need to call her."

"Yeah, but with one phone call do you call your daughter or your lawyer?"

I'll have the lawyer call Tashera, Sheila thought. *But would he be able to explain what happened the way I would,*

would he be able to explain to her why I did this...that it was for her?

Chapter 15

Mike pulled up to the house where his girlfriend of the moment lived. When he stepped out the car, Ahmed switched into the driver's seat.

"You going to see Tashera?" Mike asked.

"Nah, she ain't feelin' me right now."

"What's up, dog? You seem like you got a lot on your mind."

"I just got some unfinished business. Thanks for letting me hold your ride."

When Ahmed pulled off, he took out his cell phone and called Jessica. She answered on the first ring.

"Jessica, I should be there in ten minutes, come outside."

Ahmed drove to Jessica's house, but when he arrived, he saw two girls talking to Jessica. Jessica started shaking her head frantically and then one of the girls grabbed her from behind while the other opened the door. From what Ahmed could see, it looked like one of the girls sat on Jessica in the back seat. He saw one of the girls walk over to the driver's seat. She had a '23' etched on her back pocket. Ahmed watched the girls pull off with Jessica inside the car.

Ahmed drove back to Mike's girlfriend's house and knocked on the door. Tiffany opened it.

"Man, that was quick," Tiffany said.

"Can you send Mike out here? I really need to talk to him," Ahmed said. He began pacing.

Mike came to the door.

"Dawg, you could have taken longer than that. What was that like ten minutes?"

"Man, walk with me for a minute."

"For what? I'm tryna get into some skins."

"Mike," Ahmed yelled, "just walk with me."

As they walked toward the car and onto the sidewalk, Ahmed began to speak. His lips quivered with every word.

"Mike, somebody just snatched Jessica."

"What?"

"I just went to Jessica's house and somebody snatched her."

Ahmed grabbed his head and started shaking it.

"Slow down, slow down," Mike said. "What are you talking about? Start from the beginning."

"I just came back from Jessica's house. I drove there to get her to confess to beating down Tashera. I figured if she'd confess, Tashera could take it to the police and everything would be over. But as I'm pulling up, I see two girls talking to Jessica and they throw her into a car and pull off."

"Who do you think it was?"

"I don't know. Man, I don't know."

"I heard that Tashera's brother was like a top dog in the Deuce Trés crew. Maybe he put a hit out on Jessica," Mike said.

"Come on, man. It ain't that serious," Ahmed said.

"Think it isn't when it is? Gangs get down like that. What did the girls look like?"

"They looked like bullies, but one of the girls had the number twenty-three etched on her back pocket."

"Well Ahmed, you just solved the mystery. Twenty-three is Deuce Trés. The gang's girls snatched Jessica."

"Should I tell Tashera?"

"Man, I don't know what you should do. Leave town? That might be an option."

"Why should I leave town? I didn't do anything."

"Yeah, but you're a witness. Crews hate witnesses. And you gotta tell somebody that Jessica got snatched."

"No I don't. This is Jessica's fault. I can pretend that I never saw her tonight."

"How you gonna do that?"

"I'm not trying to get caught up in no gang business. I got a couple more months and I got a full ride to Temple University. I'm not blowing that on Jessica. She's on her own."

"That's foul, Ahmed. She could die over this."

"I ain't tryna hear that, Mike. I need a ride home. Are you gonna take me or not?"

"You're a coward, Ahmed. Find your own ride home."

"What would you do if you were me, Mike?"

"I'd go to the police."

"Before or after Deuce Trés tracked you down and killed you?"

Mike walked up the steps and back into his girlfriend's house. Ahmed pulled out his cell phone and called the last person he ever wanted to pick him up. He called his mom.

****

Khalil sat across from Lady B. Her contacts had just called her and confirmed that they had Jessica.

"What do you want to do now?" she asked.

"I need you to take me to one of the back streets by Love nightclub," Khalil said.

"Okay, let's go."

Khalil wheeled himself to Lady B's BMW. She opened the door and Khalil was able to maneuver himself into the passenger's seat. She folded his wheelchair and put it in the trunk of her car.

"How old is the girl that we snatched?" Lady B asked.

"I don't know."

"How old is your sister?"

"Seventeen. What's your point?"

"I was just wondering. Is the girl affiliated with Deuce Five?"

"Nah."

Lady B slammed her brakes and Khalil's head jutted forward.

"You mean to tell me this ain't even gang related and you snatched some teenager?"

"I gotta send a message out."

"Let me guess, the girl you snatched is either your sister's boyfriend's ex-girlfriend or ex-piece on the side. This girl found out about your sister, got mad, got jealous, and basically staged a cat fight."

"I don't know all the details. All I know is three girls jumped my sister and this girl - she is one of them. Once I spend a few minutes with her, I'll give you a full report on what really went down," Khalil said with a smirk on his face.

"I thought you learned something from what went down with you. I thought I hadn't seen you rolling with Deuce Trés because you had grown up, gotten smarter."

"What are you talking about?" Khalil asked.

"Crews and gangs—that's dead. The only reason that I did this favor for you is because we go way back, but after this I'm gone. I'm leaving this entire area. I thought when you got paralyzed you used it as your way out. But now I see that you were just looking for something to ignite your fire. You were sitting back, waiting for something to make you angry enough to get back into the crew."

"B, you need to kill this crap. You and Darren ain't never gonna leave the crew. You'll be in it until you're old and gray."

"That's where you're wrong, Khalil. We're moving. He'll be up for probation in two years. I'm starting a two-year nursing program in the fall. We realized that our lives were more important than gang banging, using drugs, selling drugs, and fighting other crews in clubs. We want to have kids. We want to be a family. Don't you want that?"

Khalil didn't say anything. He couldn't imagine anyone loving his disability enough to want to be with him for the rest of their lives. He saw himself as a burden. He felt that he'd poison any woman who dared get close enough to him. Being a part of the gang allowed him to unleash the poison on anybody who stepped in his path.

Lady B kept driving and arrived in front of a boarded up rowhouse.

"This is it."

Lady B called her girls and told them exactly where they were. Within minutes the girls arrived with Jessica. They grabbed Jessica from the back seat and walked her around the back of the abandoned house. Khalil pulled a makeshift ramp from the side of the steps. The house was filled with bottles and debris until they reached a room on the far side of the house that was completely clean and looked as if it had been remodeled. The walls were painted and the floor was carpeted. There was a futon in the room.

"Sit her down on the bed," Khalil said. "Wait outside. Tell B that I'll be out in a few minutes."

The two girls nodded at Khalil and exited the abandoned house.

Khalil looked at Jessica and snarled. "We're in the middle of nowhere," he gritted out between clenched teeth. "Nobody can hear you, so if you scream, you're wasting your breath. I'm going to take the tape off and ask you some questions. If I feel you're being real, I might let you go home tonight. Do you understand what I'm saying?"

With tears coming out of her eyes, Jessica nodded.

Khalil lifted up his sleeve and the Deuce Trés tattoo that was inked on his arm jumped under the bright light.

"Why did you attack my sister?" Khalil asked. Then Khalil's phone rang. The Caller ID read GREATER SOUTHEAST COMMUNITY HOSPITAL.

"Hello?"

"Khalil, I can't find Mommy."

Khalil rolled away from Jessica.

"What do you mean?"

"She didn't go to work today. I called her cell phone and I called the house. She hasn't answered any of the phones. I don't know what's going on. But I'm really scared. What if something has happened to her?"

"Don't worry. I'm on my way."

Khalil grabbed the tape and recovered Jessica's mouth. He rolled out of the room and secured the door with a padlock.

He left the house and wen*

"Take me to Greate   ital. Something else is going dov

Khalil got in the car a

Khalil rubbed his han with thought. *Maybe Deuce F entire family. I gotta call the o*

Chapter 16

Detective Stewart met with Mr. Ryland in his office at the police station.

"Mr. Ryland, thanks for coming and sitting with DeCalia. You can go home now. Her mother is here."

"Where is she?"

"She's in a cell for assault."

"What?"

"I informed her that DeCalia was here, and she expressed no interest in talking with her. DeCalia is being brought up here now. If you want to stick around, you can. Otherwise, I'm going to try to talk to her."

"I'll stay."

DeCalia walked into the room with a uniformed policeman.

"Where's my mom?"

"She doesn't want to see you."

"You're lying."

"No, I'm not. I told her what you're accused of, and she turned her back on you."

"Mr. Ryland, he's lying, isn't he? Isn't he?" DeCalia stood and pushed the table against the wall with force.

"No, DeCalia.

"Sit down, DeCalia," Detective Stewart said. "Your mom not wanting to see you is not the worst of your problems."

DeCalia sat and fought the tears that were about to betray her tough-girl image.

"The lab results are back. The blood on your boots matches Tashera Odom. I've already talked to the prosecutor and you're going to be tried as an adult."

DeCalia started to bite her lip.

Detective Stewart leaned over the desk and stared into DeCalia's eyes. "You're gonna take all of this heat by yourself?" he asked. "You're brave 'cause you could be in jail for ten to twenty years all by yourself. Think about that for a while."

He left the room.

Mr. Ryland moved toward DeCalia and sat.

"DeCalia," he said, "I know you think it's cool to be hard and all that. But it ain't cool. This is a serious problem. You and your friends put somebody in the hospital. When Detective Stewart comes back, you need to tell him what happened. Your mama ain't coming in to save you."

In her lowest voice possible, DeCalia said, "Okay, I will."

****

Dressed in her nightgown, Tashera got up and hobbled on crutches over to the nurse's station.

She looked down at the tag of the nurse on duty. "Miss Laraine?"

Nurse Laraine looked up from her newspaper. "Do you need anything?" she asked.

"I need to see if my mother has been admitted," she asked the nurse on duty. "Can you help me with that?"

"Did she have surgery scheduled?"

"No. I haven't been able to reach her all day and she hasn't been here. I don't know where to look."

Tears started to fall from Tashera's eyes.

"What's her name?" Nurse Laraine asked.

"Sheila. Sheila Odom."

"I'll look everywhere we have for her and I'll let you know what I find. I'm going to help you back to your room now." Nurse Laraine stood and held one of Tashera's arms. Tashera fell into her arms and started crying.

"It'll be okay," Nurse Laraine said as she patted Tashera's back. "It'll be okay."

Once Tashera returned to her room, she began to think about Ahmed. She missed talking to him. She knew that he'd have something to say to console her. She stared at the phone on her nightstand. She remembered just last week how she and Ahmed talked about getting away from Southeast. Ahmed bounced a basketball and Tashera sat watching him.

"When we go to Temple, it's gonna be off the chain," Ahmed said.

"We? I don't recall them giving me a scholarship."

"You know you're gonna be able to get in."

"You ever think about how our lives would be different if we weren't living in Southeast?"

"Yeah, all the time."

"Does the violence ever scare you?" Tashera asked.

"Yeah. If you didn't have to finish your senior year in high school, could you leave Southeast?"

Tashera shrugged. "I don't think I could leave my mother and brother behind."

"I could. We came here because my mom would make more money. We didn't hear anything about getting shot in the middle of the schoolyard. Money's not more important than safety." Ahmed dribbled the ball and spun it on his finger. "I could *definitely* leave my family behind. Walking in fear is not what I signed up for."

Tashera's conversation with Ahmed rang in her ears loudly. Violence came to her without a warning, with no reason, and as she sat in her bed, she wondered if her mother's disappearance had violent ties.

****

Khalil had tried his mother's cell phone and the house phone several times since his conversation with Tashera. His mother never left them without a word of where she was going. When he arrived in Tashera's room, she was asleep but had left her tablet open. Tashera had written a letter to somebody.

Miss Yasmin,

My brother used to be in a gang. People say once you're in a gang, you're never out. But, that's not true. When my brother was shot in the back, he got paralyzed, and all the gang members treated him like some kind of leper. They didn't invite him to go to the clubs with them anymore. They wouldn't ride him to Haynes Point. It was like they had used him and now they were done with him. He could tell that the crew wasn't feeling him anymore and so he started to stay at home all the time. That was a good thing because I got to hang out with him and do stuff with him. When he was in the gang, I never got time to be with him. We didn't get to play video games. We didn't have snack time. I know snack time seems whack, but me and my brother like a lot of the same kinds of sweets (oatmeal crème pies for example.) Right now, he's getting back in the gang, but I don't want him to 'cause for all I see they are a bunch of users. They use you up and then that's it. My brother was paralyzed during a robbery for his crew. It's not like he didn't get injured on the job. (That's my social studies talking.) I love my brother a lot. His gang almost took him away from me once. I don't want them to take him away from me again. In your book, you talk about family a little. What can I say to make my brother stop being a part of his gang?

Your girl,
Tashera

    Khalil wiped the tears from his eyes and closed Tashera's notebook. The gang was a part of who he was, and even for the love of Tashera, he wasn't sure he was ready to let it go.

Chapter 17

Friday, April 6
Four days after the attack

Tashera had awakened and found her brother asleep at the foot of her bed.

Tashera's doctor entered her room. "Tashera, it's good to see you up," Dr. Elliot said.

Khalil lifted his head and looked at the doctor.

"Good morning," Tashera said.

"I have good news for you today," the doctor said and walked over to listen to Tashera's heartbeat. "Your heart sounds strong."

"When can I leave?"

The doctor lifted Tashera's left arm slowly.

"How does that feel?" Dr. Elliot asked.

"It hurts. But not as much as it did yesterday."

"Good, good. Let me look at your stitches."

The doctor removed the bandage on Tashera's forehead. The cut had healed faster than usual.

"Tashera, what are you eating?" Dr. Elliot asked. "Your body is telling me that you're ready to go home."

"Thank you, Jesus! I gotta find my mom."

"What do you mean?"

"I called her yesterday and she didn't answer her phone. Something may have happened at work. I should hear from her today."

"I hope so. Your mother is your legal guardian and we can't release you unless she comes to pick you up."

"What about me?" Khalil asked. "I could take her home. I'm twenty-two and I'm her brother."

"The paperwork has Sheila Odom listed. Let's try to track down your mother first and go from there. It's still early yet. She'll probably be here by lunchtime."

Tashera lay back in her bed. For some reason, she didn't believe that she'd see her mother by lunchtime.

****

Ahmed sat in his Spanish class five minutes before the bell was scheduled to ring. He wondered how his relationship with Tashera would weather all the things surrounding her attack.

Alexandra timidly approached him.

"Ahmed?" she said.

Ahmed looked up and cocked his head to the side. "What? Do I know you?"

"I'm a friend of Jessica's."

"And?"

"I can't find her. I called her cell phone and she won't pick up. She told me that she was going to see you last night. Do you know what's with her?"

"I didn't see her last night, change of plans."

"Oh." Alexandra backed away and walked out the door with her shoulders hunched over. None of the typical swagger she embodied when with DeCalia and Jessica surfaced. Now that she was alone, Alexandra dwarfed back to the same insecure person she was before she met DeCalia.

A few minutes later, Mike walked in and took his usual seat next to Ahmed.

"Did you think some more about what happened last night?" Mike asked.

"Nah. I'm trying to forget everything."

"You gotta do the right thing. Make an anonymous call if you don't want to talk to the po-po directly."

"I hear you. I hear you," Ahmed said.

"Are you gonna do it?"

"It might already be too late."

"You can't think like that. Do it now. Make a call from the office. They won't know it was you."

"Mike, I appreciate what you're saying, but I ain't up to that right now. Jessica got herself into the situation. I hope she can get herself out."

"Jessica didn't know Tashera's family was down with Deuce Trés."

"And whose problem is that?"

"It's not yours. I get it." Mike got up and moved away from Ahmed.

****

Sheila Odom sat in a small gray room with a wobbly metal table and cold metal chairs. Detective Stewart walked in.

"I guess I should have put you under surveillance, huh?" he asked.

"I need to call my lawyer," Sheila said.

"When I first met you, I was concerned that you had an anger management problem. But this is worst than anger management. Do you realize what you've done?"

Sheila didn't respond.

"You have committed assault against another human being. No matter the reason, you're going to be looking at a minimum of ten years."

"I told you, y'all weren't protecting my daughter. I had to."

"Going to Anita Thomas's house? That's how you're protecting your daughter? Potentially losing your freedom for ten years, that's protecting your daughter? Sheila, what about the fact that Tashera is in the hospital right now? She probably is scared to death wondering where you are. She might need you to sign off on some procedure in the hospital, but you can't do that 'cause you in here. Tell me again how your actions helped your daughter."

"You know where you can go, right?"

"You know, Sheila," Detective Stewart said before sitting in a chair across the table from Sheila, "I visit middle schools in DC talking to the kids about the dangers of making bad decisions and of letting their anger get the best of them. I bet you're a real good mom, but this problem that you've created is not going away. If Anita Thomas decides to press charges against you, and I see no reason why she shouldn't, you're facing hard time in the penitentiary."

Detective Stewart stood and walked to the door. "I truly hope your decision to go to that woman's house was worth not being able to return to your own house for the next ten years." Opening the door, he called out, "Officer Fedder, stand over here while Ms. Odom makes her phone call."

Detective Stewart pointed to a phone that was at the edge of the table.

"You can call your attorney on that phone."

Detective Stewart could barely look at Sheila. Instead of being able to focus on solving Tashera's case, he'd be handing over information to the prosecution in their case against Sheila Odom.

****

Anita Thomas spent the night in Greater Southeast Community Hospital. She didn't have a clear recollection of how she even got there, but she remembered talking to Detective Stewart about Sheila Odom coming to her house.

That woman was like some kind of crazed madwoman, Anita thought.

Detective Stewart had tried to explain Sheila's situation.

"She came to your house because she believes your daughter jumped hers," he said.

"DeCalia didn't have anything to do with that," Anita said.

"Spoken like a true mother. But unfortunately that's not true. The reports are back from the lab. It is Tashera's blood that was on the tip of your daughter's shoe. How do you explain that?"

Anita felt a sharp pain in her chest as her memory failed her. After taking a few quick breaths, she closed her eyes and tried to grasp any images, words regarding what happened.

Sheila Odom splayed across her mind. She recalled that the girl her daughter was accused of attacking was in a hospital in DC. With any luck, she'd be at this one.

Anita grunted as she pulled herself from the bed and shuffled across the room, determined to see if she could find out if the Odom daughter was located in the hospital.

****

At the nurse's station, Nurse Laraine organized folders. She nodded and said "Hi" to a passing nurse, and her eyes took in *The Washington Post* that rested on the counter. A headline read, "Two Barry High Mothers Caught in Fistfight."

She placed the folders on the counter, snatched up the newspaper, and began reading the article. She grabbed the paper and rushed into Tashera's room.

"Tashera, how are you this morning?" Nurse Laraine asked.

"Still worried."

"I think I found your mother."

"Where? Where is she?"

"I think she's at the DC jail. Read this article."

Nurse Laraine handed Tashera the paper. Khalil rolled his wheelchair toward the bed.

Tashera's eye opened wide. "Khalil," she said, her voice in near hysterics, "Mom's in jail! She got into a fight with a mother of one of the girls who jumped me."

"Let me see the paper," Khalil said.

Khalil read through the article as fast as he could.

"Nurse Laraine," Tashera said, "the doctor said I'd be released today if my mom came to pick me up. But it doesn't look like she'll be able to. My brother's twenty-two. Can I just go home with him?"

"Let me get your paperwork started."

Tashera started to get dressed. The first thing on her agenda would be to see about their mother.

Chapter 18

Ashe read the morning's paper and decided to visit Tashera in the hospital before his shift started.

When Ashe knocked on Tashera's hospital door, he was surprised to see Khalil there.

Ashe attended Barry High when Khalil was still a student. He remembered that Khalil terrorized everybody in the school—students and teachers alike, including him. None of the students stood up to members of the Deuce Trés gang. They knew if they even hesitated that the gang would be waiting for them when school was over to make them a part of the pavement.

"Hey," Ashe said.

"You look familiar," Tashera and Khalil said at the same time.

"I found you on the street. I told the girls to stop kicking you."

"Good lookin'," Khalil said.

Ashe walked over to Khalil. "We went to school together," he said.

Khalil grabbed his shades out of pouch on his chair and put them on. Khalil knew that anybody who wasn't a member of Deuce Trés he threatened, beat up, or otherwise made their lives miserable.

"I know your mother is down at the jail," Ashe said. "I stopped by in case you needed anything."

"You tryna push up on my sister?"

Ashe stepped back. "Nothing like that. I just know it's crazy right now. I was just tryin' to look out."

"Khalil, stop trippin'," Tashera said. "As a matter fact, we could use a ride down to the jail. We need to see her."

"Have you been released yet?"

"Yeah, " Tashera said, "but we didn't have a ride."

Ashe looked at Khalil who was still trying to analyze him, then turned his attention back to Tashera.

"Now you do," he said. "Let's go."

****

Lenise Barnes walked into the police station and bumped into Detective Rodriguez.

"I'm sorry, I'm sorry, Ma'am," Lenise said.

"It's okay. Is there something that I can help you with?"

"My daughter, Jessica Barnes is missing. I want to find her."

"How old is she?"

"Sixteen."

"We have a lot of teen runaways. Has she runaway before?"

"No."

"Did you all have a fight or anything the last time that you saw her?"

"Not at all. In fact, she was so happy she told me that one of her friends was stopping by, and I went upstairs and fell asleep," Lenise Barnes said.

"Then what happened?"

"I don't think she ever came back into the house. She didn't turn off the lights in her bedroom. She didn't take her cell phone. I don't know what happened to her. "

"How long has it been since the last time that you saw her?"

"It was last night."

"It generally has to be at least 24 hours before we consider somebody missing."

"Look, I don't want to waste your time, but something is going on with her. For the past three or four days, she's been acting really strange. She started whispering when I walk into a room. I had planned to talked to her friends, perhaps head over to Marion Berry High and talk to the principal."

"Follow me to my office, and I'll write up a report."

More calamity at Marion Barry High, Detective Rodriguez thought. *Is any learning going on over there?*

****

Alexandra had been calling Jessica's phone since last night. Jessica had told Alexandra that Ahmed was stopping by her house. Alexandra never understood why Jessica was so crazy about Ahmed. He was just a pointy-headed basketball player to her.

Alexandra dressed slowly for school. She knew DeCalia was in jail, and she had begun to worry that something had happened to Jessica.

Jessica never took the Deuce Trés threat seriously, Alexandra thought. *I tried to tell her. They've probably killed her. I know I'm next.*

Alexandra got on the bus and went to school as usual. In front of the school, she looked around for any sign of DeCalia or Jessica. She didn't see any. She visited the bathroom where she, DeCalia, and Jessica hung out before third period. Her girls never showed up.

A couple of girls came into the bathroom and saw Alexandra leaning by the window.

"Get out of here, skank," one of the girls said. The others laughed. "You ain't nothin' without your girls wit' you. Not so tough without your little crew. We oughta beat you down right now."

Alexandra balled her hands into tight fists and was prepared to defend herself if it came down to a battle. When she walked passed one of the girls, she was punched hard in the arm. Alexandra just looked at the five girls and kept walking.

Alexandra walked into her first period class and sat there with her head down the entire time. When the bell rang, she got up and walked to the principal's office.

"Miss Cannon," she said, "I haven't seen Jessica today? Is she on the sick list?"

"You know I'm not supposed to share that information."

"Please Miss Cannon, I'm worried about her." Tears formed in the corners of her eyes.

Miss Cannon opened up a notebook on her desk and looked over the names of the students who had called in the absentee line.

"Jessica Barnes nor her family members called in today."

"Thank you, Miss Cannon."

"Is there something wrong, Alexandra?"

"Everything and nothing."

"What are you talking about?"

"Don't worry, Miss Cannon. I just realized that I should have done this a long time ago."

"What are you talking about?"

"See you later, Miss Cannon. And no matter what other people say, you are the best dressed teacher or administrator, you know what I'm saying, in this school."

"Thanks, Alexandra."

Alexandra moped through her classes as an overwhelming sense of dread tugged at her insides.

Meeting DeCalia and Jessica had made Alexander virtually invincible; she was feared and admired, but now, she couldn't help but to remember the last time she had felt so empty and open to pain.

In the sixth grade, Alexandra wore her hair in long French braids. She liked dresses and proper clothes. But in the middle of the sixth grade, some girls who didn't like dresses started to pay attention to Alexandra. They started to poke her in the ribs in class when the teachers weren't looking. They'd trip her when she carried her lunch tray in the cafeteria.

Alexandra went home and told her parents about how she was picked on in school and they told her, "Alexandra, you gotta stop being so picky and do a better job of getting along with the other girls."

"I don't want to go to this school anymore," Alexandra cried.

"We can't fight your battles for you, Alexandra," her mother said.

In sixth grade, Alexandra just started to feel what it was like to be targeted by hateful girls. In the seventh grade, the behavior got worse. She was spat on, taunted, and even her shorts were pulled down in gym class in front of her male classmates. Alexandra went to her parents again and told them.

"I'm hated in that school. Put me any place but there," Alexandra said.

"You're either gonna sink or swim, Alexandra," her father said, "What are you gonna do?"

Alexandra wanted to become invisible. She didn't want anyone to see her. Sixth grade seemed so far from where she was as an eleventh grader. Alexandra wished she had someone to talk to about what she felt. She was afraid. But she knew her parents would be telling her the same thing they'd told her since sixth grade, "We're not gonna fight your battles for you. You gotta figure this stuff out for yourself."

Alexandra hadn't always made the best choices for herself; she realized that. One more mistake wouldn't hurt.

****

DeCalia sat in front of Detective Stewart as her arms shook.

"Are you ready to tell me what happened?" Detective Stewart asked.

DeCalia nodded.

"First of all, I ain't no rat."

Detective Stewart put both hands in front of his face.

"If a hammer is gonna fall, I want it to fall on me," she continued. "It was my idea. I inflicted the damage. It's all on me."

"What happened?"

"This girl stole my girl's boyfriend. I didn't think too highly of it, so I started a fight with her. Some of my friends were there, but they were just watching. They didn't have anything to do with it."

"DeCalia, I can't believe you are sitting here lying to my face."

"What are you talking about?" DeCalia asked.

"We have eyewitnesses that saw more than one person hitting Tashera. So, you can't say you're the only person who did anything."

"Your eyewitness is wrong. I kicked her in the head, in the ribs. I threw her to the ground. My friends were there, but they were on the sidelines. And you can ask them, they'll tell you the truth."

"Who are your friends?"

"Jessica Barnes and Alexandra Kent. But they ain't never been in no trouble, so outside of asking them a few questions, you shouldn't even bring them in here like this."

"You're really loyal, aren't you, DeCalia?"

"Death before dishonor," DeCalia said.

"You said it was your idea?"

"Yeah, my girl Jessica, she ain't the fighting type. So when I heard about the situation, I just came up with the whole thing."

"This is your story, huh, DeCalia?"

"Yep."

"You gonna soldier ten to twenty years on your own? Do you think your mom would want you to do this?"

"Obviously, she don't care or she'd be here." Two tears rolled down DeCalia's cheeks.

"You act like you don't care if you're in jail, outta jail, walking free, or in a casket."

"I don't care. I don't know what caring is."

Detective Stewart stepped away from the room. He couldn't bear to see young people accept prison time as if it was a trip to Six Flags. He knew DeCalia would live to regret the statements that she made today.

Chapter 19

Sheila decided to call her cousin, Richard King, a successful attorney with a Georgetown law practice. Sheila never really liked Richard. He always stood apart from the rest of the family. At the family reunions, while all the cousins sat back, drank beer, and played cards, he just sat, listened to their conversations, and drank bottled water. He didn't use the slang that their other family members used either. Sheila thought he talked like he was in an English class every minute of the day.

At a recent family gathering, she told him, "You need to loosen up. Have a drink."

"I am loose," he said.

"It doesn't seem like it."

"Why is that? 'Cause I'm not passed out in a chair in the corner with slobber hanging out of my mouth? What right do you have to tell me when I'm loose or not? We're related, but you don't know me that well."

"See Rich, that's why the family stays away from your corny behind. You always gotta put somebody down."

"You need to get a grip. You came over here telling me to have a drink despite the fact that alcohol messes with my diabetes. No, you don't know about that, but that doesn't stop you from making suggestions."

"Your problem is you think you're better than everybody else in the family."

"No, the problem is that's what you think."

His words stung Sheila like vinegar in an open wound.

No one in her family was as successful as Rich was. He attended the family reunions like everyone else, but at the end of the day, most of the family saw him as an outcast and talked about him negatively. Her uncle Pete often told her, "Rich is just trying to be like those white boys—with his talk and all that. But he's black just like the rest of us."

Sheila dialed information and was connected to Richard's law firm.

"Can I speak to Richard King, please?"

"Who's calling?"

"This is his cousin, Sheila. It's an emergency."

"He's not available at this moment. But…"

"I said it was an emergency."

"Sheila, I mean you no harm, but we get clients who have emergencies every fifteen minutes in our office. Tell me the emergency and I'll get the information to him as soon as possible."

"I'm in jail," Sheila said and took in a deep breath.

"Which one?"

"The seventh district."

"What have you been charged with?"

"Assault. I've been here overnight, but I think if I had a lawyer, they'd let me go to court so I could be out on bail or something. I'm not really sure, but I think so."

"You want Richard to represent you?"

"Yeah, that's why I'm calling."

"I'll let him know. Hold on for a moment," the receptionist said.

After a few moments, Richard said, "Hello, Sheila."

"Hey, Richard."

"My assistant just filled me in on the details. Who did you allegedly assault?"

"The mother of a girl who attacked your little cousin."

"I'll be down to the station as soon as possible."

"Okay. Thanks, Richard," Sheila said and was escorted back to the holding cell.

****

Detective Rodriguez tapped lightly on Detective Stewart's door.

"You got a minute?" Detective Rodriguez asked.

"Sure."

"I gotta a hunch—a sort of bad feeling."

"About what?"

"I just took a missing persons report from Lenise Barnes," Detective Rodriguez said and paused. She let the words hang in the air for a moment.

"Am I supposed to know who that is?" Detective Stewart asked.

"Did DeCalia Thomas name her accomplices in the attack on Tashera Odom?"

"Yes and No."

"Huh?"

"DeCalia claims that the entire attack was all her. She claims every punch, kick, and hit came from her. All she says is she had two friends who were there, but that the friends didn't get involved. They watched; innocent spectators, if you will."

"What are the other two girls' names?"

Detective Stewart looked through his notes.

"Alexandra Kent and Jessica Barnes."

"Well, Jessica Barnes is now missing."

Detective stood. "What is going on in this city?"

"I don't think it's a coincidence. Gangs are known for creating missing persons," Detective Rodriguez said.

"Yeah, maybe it's time to talk to Tashera's brother. He's the link to Deuce Trés."

****

Ahmed called Tashera's cell phone. He didn't have the confidence to tell the police what he saw, but he could tell Tashera.

"Hello?"

"Tashera, I really need to speak with you."

"I can't right now. I'm on my way to see my mom."

"I apologize for everything. I love you and I'm sorry that I hurt you."

"I love you, too, Ahmed. I'll call you when I get back home."

"You're out of the hospital?"

"Yeah, I just got out. I'll be home though for a few days before I can go back to school."

"I'm just glad you're feeling better. Don't forget to call me."

"I won't. I promise."

Chapter 20

Anita Thomas strolled into Tashera's hospital room and looked around. *It doesn't look like anybody had this room,* she thought. She walked to the nurse's station.

"I'm looking for Miss Odom, the young lady who was in this room," Anita said.

"Oh. You're too late. She and her brother just left to see their mom at the courthouse. They seem liked a real close knit family."

Dang. I wanted to see that little hussy for myself, Anita thought.

"When I spoke with her, she seemed like such a nice lady," the nurse said. "I know she loves her daughter. Hopefully the court will be kind to her."

"Not if I have anything to do with it," Anita mumbled under her breath.

****

As Khalil rode in the back of the ambulance with his wheelchair strapped in place so he wouldn't move, he looked at his watch. It had been more than twelve hours since his girls had kidnapped one of Tashera's attackers. He thought about how tight the duct tape should have been around her wrists. He wondered if she'd be able to wriggle herself free.

She looked really scared, he thought. *How long will I have to sit in the police station with my mom?* He hated police stations. And his work wasn't done with Tashera's attacker. He hoped that he'd be able to get out of the police station and the courthouse sooner rather than later.

****

Two offices escorted DeCalia to a cold room in the police station. Cousin Fran, Detective Stewart, Mr. Ryland, Attorney Langford Dempsey, and Community Prosecutor Wellesley were all waiting for her.

She was still wearing the clothes that she had on when she was first arrested at school.

DeCalia looked at Fran who sat at the end of the black metal table.

"Where's my muva?" DeCalia asked.

"We haven't been able to reach her," Mr. Ryland said.

"I'm Community Prosecutor Wellesley. I handle the juvenile cases in Ward 7. We were just telling Miss Sellers that our cases are backed up in the courts, and we'll be moving you to Oak Hill, a maximum security juvenile detention facility that houses inmates 14 to 21 while you await your trial."

DeCalia looked away from Prosecutor Wellesley.

"DeCalia, I'm Attorney Langford Dempsey..."

"Did your mama give you that name?" DeCalia chuckled.

"I'm here to represent you and make sure that your rights aren't violated since your parental guardian is not present."

"I'm seventeen. I can handle it."

Mr. Ryland stood. "Everyone except Fran, I need a moment to speak with this student, please."

Everyone cleared the room.

"I know you think it's cool to be all hard and act like none of this phases you, but DeCalia, this is serious," he began. "Detective Stewart told me that you claimed you attacked Tashera Odom on your own. We all know that's not true, but I understand you don't want to be a rat—I get that. But why must you act like you don't care if you throw your own life away? You act like your life means nothing."

"It doesn't. My own muva can't come down to sit with me while I'm in here, so obviously I'm a waste of space."

"I don't know what your mother is doing, but I do know, if you give up on yourself, you'll never get over it."

"You win. I've already given up."

"I don't win when I see students like you give up. I lose you to the system. Understand that you're about to be put in a run-down facility with people who are harder than you, who have more hatred than you, who are badder than you. You think you bad? You're going to meet somebody in Oak Hill that'll make this beating on Tashera look like a kindergarten fight. Fight for yourself. It's not about what your mother is doing for you. Make this prosecutor want to give you another chance. Sometimes our parents aren't there for us when we need them to be, but like you said, you're seventeen. You should want to do better for yourself."

"Are you done?"

Mr. Ryland bit his lip. "For now."

Mr. Ryland opened the door and everyone else came in.

"If there's nothing further, we're going to transport DeCalia now," Detective Stewart said. DeCalia walked out of the room without saying good-bye. The two officers loaded her on to a DC Department of Corrections bus. She sat at the first seat available and looked straight ahead.

****

Ashe looked over at Tashera who sat in the passenger seat of his ambulance. "Do you like school?" he asked.

Tashera looked through the window behind her and saw Khalil staring through it at her. "I used to."

"When did you stop liking it?"

"When I got jumped."

"Did you know the girls who jumped you?"

"No, but apparently they knew me. One of them or all of 'em, I don't know—they like or used to like my boyfriend."

"Girls—even when I was in high school—were quick to fight over a guy."

"It's stupid to me—even with my own situation. My boyfriend told me that he dissed one of the girls and so months later, she's after me. For what? It wasn't like I was wit' him when he was dating her. It's stupid, but it's just how it is."

"It's probably always gonna be that way."

"Yeah, that's why I'll be carrying around a switchblade from now on."

"You can't be serious," Ashe said.

Tashera turned to him and twisted her neck. "Why ain't I? If you hadn't seen me that day, I might be still lying in that parking lot. What am I supposed to do? Continue to be a victim?"

"No, but you can't change who you are either. Believe me, if you walk around carrying a switchblade everyday, you're gonna find a way to use it."

"Before this situation, I would have never thought I'd be the person to carry a knife, but everything has changed. Nobody can tell me anything right now about minding your own business or being non-violent, so save your Martin Luther King speech. I was attacked because some girl didn't like me because of who my boyfriend was. I ain't never gonna forget that."

"I'm not asking you to forget. I'm asking you to be better than the girls who attacked you."

"For what?"

"Because you're better than they are. You don't need to sink to their level."

"Once I get to their level, I'll let you know if I need it or not," Tashera said and got out of the ambulance the minute it stopped in front of the police station.

Ashe unhooked Khalil and lowered him out of the ambulance.

"I can go in with y'all to help you navigate," Ashe said.

"Nah, that's okay," Khalil said.

"Khalil, it'll help us get to Mommy faster."

Ashe put on the ambulance's hazard lights and walked into Detective Stewart's office. He was not there. Ashe walked a few doors down and tapped on Detective Rodriguez's door.

"This is Tashera Odom," he said. "She's looking for her mother. Can you help her?"

"Yeah, no problem."

Tashera turned around and extended her hand toward Ashe.

"Thank you for saving my life."

"You're welcome, but rethink what we just talked about. You don't really want to go down that road," Ashe said and left the police station.

"Sit down for a moment," Detective Rodriguez said, "I'll help you locate your mother." Once Tashera was seated, Rodriquez asked, "Are you here by yourself?"

"No, my brother is with me."

"Where is he?"

"He's probably in the hallway."

Detective Rodriguez went to her door and looked up the hallway. She didn't see anybody.

"I don't see him."

"Why are you more worried about my brother than my mom? I'm here to see my mom."

Detective Rodriguez sat.

"My fault. I'll call down to holding and have her brought to a room where you two can talk to her."

I can't wait, Tashera thought. The newspaper had painted her mother as some kind of lunatic who went crazy whenever her daughter got into minor scrapes. The newspaper had Sheila attacking Anita with villainous force and hatred. Tashera had never seen her mother as angry as she had been portrayed in the paper.

Who was my mother really? Tashera began to wonder.

Chapter 21

Jessica lay in the bed with her hands tied behind her back and her feet bound at the ankles. She had slept through the night though she heard gunshots off and on. Gunshots weren't new background noise to a DC native.

Now that Jessica had awakened, she had tried to use her shoulders to lift the duct tape from the corner of her mouth. Her cotton shirt just smoothed over the duct tape. She spit into the duct tape and lay on one side. She hoped the moisture would loosen the tape. She had planned to scream and believed that somebody would hear her.

When Jessica closed her eyes, she could see her and her friends attacking Tashera. None of this would have happened if she hadn't initiated the attack.

I'm so stupid, Jessica thought.

But she was just as angry as she was stupid.

Jessica couldn't get Ahmed out of her system. After Ahmed passed her around to the basketball team, she had to look at him and his teammates everyday. They were laughing at her. They all were laughing at her. After Ahmed dumped Jessica, she couldn't get a good night's sleep. She'd wake up with nightmares of Ahmed forcing her to have sex with strangers on the street. She'd have nightmares that someone on the team gave her a venereal disease. She started trying to stay up all night. Jessica was willing to do anything to stop having nightmares.

A month before the attack on Tashera, Jessica visited a palm reader at a Fall Festival in Northern Virginia.

111

"You are deeply troubled," the palmist told her. "You must get to the root. You will not be happy if you don't kill the root."

Jessica walked away from the palmist. Ahmed was the root of her problems. His mistreatment of her led her to have nightmares, to doubt herself, and to walk around looking like a zombie.

I wanted to kill Ahmed, Jessica remembered.

But a conversation with her mother shortly after meeting the palmist changed the course of Jessica's actions.

"What's been up with you lately?" her mother asked. "You seem all gloom and doom?"

"Yeah, that's me."

"You got man problems?"

"Something like that. I need to pay somebody back."

"A guy?"

"Yeah," Jessica said.

"Though their hearts aren't always easy to find, the way to hurt a man is through his heart."

Jessica carried her mother's words around with her like she had memorized a scripture from the bible. Then one day when she was getting ready to get on the bus, she saw Ahmed and Tashera. They were laughing about something. Ahmed was laughing with her with admiration and love in his eyes. The way he touched her waist and reached out to hold her hand, anyone who watched could have seen that Ahmed was in love with her.

Jessica knew instantly that the girl who Ahmed was laughing with, that was the girl who was his heart.

Jessica shook the thoughts of Ahmed from her head. It wasn't time to think of him. She realized that she spent too much time thinking about him. She needed to find a way to save herself.

****

After sitting in Detective Rodriguez's office for more than twenty minutes, Tashera's ribs began to throb in pain.

"They're takin' forever," Khalil said. "I can't stand police."

"We're just trying to get through this, K, that's all." Tashera turned to him. "Where were you when I first came back here?"

"I was talking to Ashe. You know we went to high school together."

"And you remember him?"

"Nah, he was some square that I beat up probably." Khalil laughed.

"That ain't funny. I'm a square. You ever think the reason I got attacked is for some karma from your gang banging days?"

Khalil would never admit it, but that's exactly what he felt. Those feelings motivated his need for revenge.

"You tryna blame me?" he asked. "I would never let anyone hurt you."

"You wouldn't knowingly, but don't you think somebody gotta pay for all the pain you've sent into the universe? Somebody gotta pay and maybe that somebody is me."

Khalil started to wheel himself out of the office when Detective Rodriguez walked back in.

"Tashera, sorry for taking so long," the detective said. "Is this your brother?"

"Yes."

"Hi, I'm Detective Rodriguez. You must be Khalil."

"How you know my name? You got an FBI file on me?"

"Why would I have a file on you?"

"I don't know, you tell me."

"To answer your question, Khalil, I spoke with your mother prior to this incident, so she told me that she had a son named Khalil. Sorry my answer isn't laced with conspiracies."

"Whatever," Khalil said.

"When I first called down to holding, your mother was in the process of being moved to the courthouse to be arraigned. I thought we could get a moment to speak with her, but they went ahead and moved her. I'm on my way to the courthouse now, so you can ride with me, if you like."

"Is your car wheelchair friendly?" Khalil asked.

"Yeah, we'll be able to manage. Anyway, this will give me time to speak with you and Tashera. Give me one moment."

Detective Rodriguez left her office and stopped by Detective Stewart's office.

"I'm getting ready to ride down to the courthouse with the Odom kids," she said. "You up for the ride?"

Detective Stewart's eyes widened. "Are you kidding? The president couldn't bribe me from this car trip. Make sure it's the longest ride to the courthouse in history."

"Absolutely," Detective Rodriguez said.

Chapter 22

Anita Thomas sat in the back of the courtroom and listened to the court cases. There were thefts, carjackings, assaults, and all of the prosecutors wanted to nail all the defendants to the wall. Anita noticed that the accused people who dressed well got better treatment than the people who came before the judge in the state issued prison garb. One of Anita's middle school teachers had told her once that clothing says a lot about a person. In the courthouse it decided if you're going back to lock-up or if you'd be out on bond.

Anita's phone rang. She saw her cousin Fran's number on her Caller ID. Anita stepped out of the courtroom and answered.

"Where are you, Anita?' Fran asked.

"I'm in the courthouse," she replied.

"For what?"

"Ima make sure that trick who attacked me doesn't get out on bond."

"Oh. Calia could have used you here today. They just sent her to Oak Hill."

"They can't do that without me there."

"It's already done. They not waitin' for late parents. She's gone. She's already on the bus."

"Well, I did tell her one time that I'd never visit her in jail."

"You kept your promise. Are you gonna meet me at the house to check on Li'l Tommy?"

"Not right now. I told you I got bid'ness in the courthouse. I'll check on Tommy after I handle this."

Anita hung up the phone and returned to the courtroom.

****

In a small interview room within the Superior Court Building, Sheila sat across from her cousin Richard.

"Thanks for coming, cuz," Sheila said.

Richard leaned forward slightly and splayed his hands along the table. "Tell me what happened."

"I went to Anita Thomas' house looking for her daughter."

"What is her daughter's name?"

"Calia."

"Why were you looking for her daughter?"

"I wanted to ask her questions about attacking Tashera."

Richard clasped his hands together. "Why did you go to her mother's house instead of going to the school or police?"

"I talked to the police at the hospital first. Then I went to Barry High and I talked to the principal."

"What's the principal's name?"

"Sean Ryland, the one who used to play for the Bullets."

"What happened after you arrived at her home?"

"She had an attitude. She didn't want me there. She couldn't tell me anything about the attack on Tashera. So, it just got heated up in there."

"Did you go to her house with the intention of getting physical?"

"No, but whatever is whatever."

116

"What would have happened had her daughter been there?"

"I don't know. I really don't know."

Richard grabbed a black dress out of a bag that sat next to his briefcase.

"Put this dress on. It'll make the judge look more favorably upon you."

Sheila took the dress and looked at it.

"It's not my size, it's too big."

"It doesn't matter. The judge won't be checking to see if the dress fits, but you'll look better to him than the rest of the criminals who go into court in orange jumpsuits or street wear," Richard said.

"Do you think it'll be hard to get me off?"

"Right now, you're looking at an assault charge. We're going into court to see if the judge will release you on your own recognizance or if you'll have to put up bail money."

Sheila motioned that she was ready to put on the dress and Richard turned his back.

"Most judges are sympathetic to mothers who are trying to defend their children. Let's hope he sees you that way," Richard said.

****

Detective Stewart sat in the backseat of the Chevy Tahoe next to Khalil. Tashera sat in the front next to Detective Rodriguez.

"Tashera, we've made a lot of headway into your case," Detective Rodriquez said. "We believe that we're gonna get to the bottom of who did this to you. Have you talked to your boyfriend since this happened?"

"Yeah," Tashera answered.

"What's he been saying?"

"Nothing really. He's mad that it happened mostly."

Tashera knew not to say much to cops. To her, things had a funny way of being switched around and used against you when you talked to the 5-0.

"Do you think you and your boyfriend may have flaunted your relationship in front of his ex or something?"

"Where are you getting this from? I didn't have anything to do with this. I didn't provoke anybody, I don't know the girls who did it at all, so don't try to make it like it's my fault somehow."

"Most people go off for a certain reason. I wanted to know if you knew the reason."

"Yeah, they went off because they're stupid. Go ask them why they went off. Don't ask me."

"It's funny you should mention that, Tashera," Detective Stewart chimed in. "We've talked to one of the girls, but now another girl is missing." Detective Stewart looked directly at Khalil who returned a cold stare.

"What are you talking about?" Tashera asked.

"The mother of one of the girls reported her missing today."

"How you know the girl missing is one of the girls who jumped my sister?" Khalil asked.

"The ring leader named names."

"Hmm," Khalil said.

"There's a rumor going around that you're a member of Deuce Trés, Khalil," Detective Stewart said. "Is that true?"

"Nah. I'm a former member. Since I've been a wheeler, I ain't been active like that."

Detective Stewart studied Khalil's facial expressions. *If Khalil is lying, he's doing a real good job of looking truthful,* Stewart thought as he and Khalil stared each other down.

"About five or so years ago, I had a case where Deuce Trés kidnapped some members of the Deuce Five crew."

"Word?" Khalil asked.

"Every cop in the District knows that snatching people off the block is modus operandi for Deuce Trés."

"Really?"

"Yeah, really," Detective Stewart said.

"You ever think the girl who the mama say is missing, got a new man and she ran away from home 'cause she tired of hearing her mom nag her to death?" Khalil asked.

"According to her mother, the girl didn't have a boyfriend."

"You know what they say, Moms is last to know."

"Is your mother gonna be the last to know?" Detective Stewart asked.

"Last to know what?"

"Last to know that you're active again in Deuce Trés."

"Man, go ahead wit' that. My mom knows everything about me."

Detective Stewart had to admit that Khalil was fearless when it came to their conversation. Khalil didn't stutter or hesitate when Detective Stewart asked him questions.

"Are we there yet?" Khalil yelled to the front of the truck.

"The Superior Court Building is at the next light," Detective Rodriguez said.

"It's about time," Tashera said faintly.

She couldn't wait to talk to her mother, and Khalil wanted to get as far away from Detective Stewart as he could.

Chapter 23

While Detectives Rodriguez and Stewart parked the truck, Tashera opted to push Khalil's wheelchair up the ramp of the Superior Court Building.

"Where do you think we should look for Mom?" Tashera asked.

"I don't know. Let's just go straight ahead," Khalil responded.

Tashera entered the building and had to stop to go through metal detectors. A security guard ran his wand around Khalil and his chair.

"Where do I go for court cases from District 7?" Tashera asked a receptionist in the front of the building just beyond the security check-in.

"Third floor."

Tashera and Khalil took the elevator, and upon stepping off it, they spotted their mother who'd been walking in the opposite direction.

"Mom," Tashera called out.

Sheila looked up with a smile wider than the ones she wore when her children opened presents on Christmas morning.

Tashera ignored the pain that ebbed inside her and raced to her mother. They pulled one another into a tight hug.

"I've been worried about you," she said. "How are you doing?"

"I'm hangin' in there," Sheila answered. "Khalil, how are you doing?" she asked and kissed her son on the forehead.

"Good. I'm good."

Richard lightly touched Sheila's arm. "Sheila, we need to get into the court room," he said. "We don't want to miss being called."

"Who's he?" Tashera asked.

"He's your cousin Richard, and he's my lawyer."

"I didn't know we had any lawyers in the family," Tashera said.

"They don't talk about me much," Richard said and looked at Sheila with a smirk.

When they walked in the courtroom, they took a seat on the left side and waited for their docket to be called. Within ten minutes, the judge called, "Docket # 959179907, Sheila Odom."

"We're present, your honor," Richard said.

"How do you plead to the charge of assault against Anita Thomas?"

"Not guilty," Sheila said.

"May I have permission to address the court?" Richard asked.

"You may," the judge said.

"My client, Ms. Odom, has no prior arrests or criminal complaints. She has been at her job for over ten years, her daughter is in high school here, and her son lives with her. She is no flight risk, so I ask that she be released on her own recognizance."

"We have no problem with that, your honor," the Community Prosecutor said.

"Hold on one minute," Anita yelled from the back of the courtroom. She stood and walked down in front of the judge.

"Can I talk, your honor?" she asked.

"Who are you?" the judge asked.

"I am Anita Thomas. She assaulted me yesterday. She came to my home and tried to kick the door in. She broke my glass table and terrorized me. I do not believe that she should be able to get out on her own. She's crazy as a loon."

The Community Prosecutor looked at Anita.

"How do you respond, counselor?"

"My client had reason to believe that Ms. Thomas' daughter had attacked her child," Richard began. "She was distraught and attempted to talk to Ms. Thomas, but Ms. Thomas was defensive, aggressive, and uncooperative. My client's personal history should weigh in on if she gets ROR. She wants to have her day in court. We believe she will be exonerated of any and all charges."

"That's some bull," Anita said.

"You need to watch your mouth in this courtroom," the judge said. "Sheila Odom is so released on her own recognizance." The judge slammed his gravel.

"It ain't over," Anita said and quickly walked passed Sheila, her attorney, and her two kids.

****

DeCalia and several other teens got off the DC Department of Corrections bus and were escorted to the front of the Oak Hill juvenile facility. The facility was bigger than a high school and had barbed wire fencing. The entire group didn't say a word.

The boys and girls were separated from each other. DeCalia and three other girls went into an area on the left side while five boys went to an area on the right. A broad-shouldered female guard who stood about five-foot-ten told the girls, "Take your clothes off" while another female guard watched in case the girls protested or tried to runaway.

One female guard pointed at DeCalia.

"You first," the guard said. "Take your clothes off."

"No," DeCalia said.

"You must be new," the short, stocky female guard said. "When you come from outside, you have to be strip searched. That's the rule. You can either take your clothes off and do it by yourself, or we'll restrain you and it'll be a whole lot worse."

DeCalia swallowed hard. She couldn't stand to change into gym shorts in the girls' locker room at Marion Barry High. How was she going to last in a place that strip searched people?

DeCalia removed her clothes, except her socks.

"Take your socks off, too," one of the guards said.

"I don't like being barefoot."

"Does it look like we're here to talk about the things you like? We're not going to tell you again."

DeCalia removed her socks and stood there, completely naked from head to toe. The shorter guard looked in DeCalia's mouth, ears and nose.

"Lift your arms," the guard said, then she checked DeCalia's armpits.

"Stick your hands out."

DeCalia did as she was told and the guard examined the space between her fingers. The guard lifted her left breast and looked underneath and did the same with the right. She showed as much warmth as a block of ice. She lifted a roll of flab that DeCalia had around her belly.

DeCalia knew she couldn't do anything. She just stood there and felt absolutely humiliated.

"Bend over and cough," the guard said.

"What? I ain't doin' that."

The big guard came over and put DeCalia in a headlock and bent her over.

"Now cough," she said.

DeCalia started crying and coughing at the same time. She could hardly breathe.

"Stand up straight," the shorter guard said and then examined the spaces between DeCalia's toes. "You're done. You can take your clothes and go in the other room and get dressed."

DeCalia had been suspended from school numerous times, had been kicked out of after school programs, summer programs, and other activities that involved other kids, but never had she been violated like she had when they forced her to show them her inner most private parts. As she put on her last piece of clothing, she realized that she had entered a place where she did not have any rights. And nobody cared what she thought about it.

****

At home, Sheila, Khalil, and Tashera sat in the living room. Since they'd been home, Khalil had been tapping his right thumb on his thigh. He seemed anxious. Whenever Tashera attempted to give Sheila eye contact, Sheila would look off into a distant place as if they weren't in the same room in the same house.

"Mom, why did you go over that woman's house?" Tashera asked.

"To defend you."

"You could go to jail."

"Tashera, stop overreacting. I'm not going anywhere. I had to send a message to that family that they can't just put their hands on my daughter and think nothing is gonna happen."

"My point exactly," Khalil said.

"What do you mean by that, Khalil?" Tashera asked.

"Nothing. Nothing. I'm just sayin' people can't think they can touch you and not pay the consequences."

"I appreciate everybody wanting to take up for me, but Mom, you could lose your job because of this. You could have been seriously hurt even. Then where would I be?"

"But I didn't get hurt, did I?" Sheila asked.

"I'm so glad you didn't get hurt, but when I read that newspaper article and all the bad things that were being said about you, I thought that you could go to a place where people would hurt you. I don't want you to go to prison trying to protect me from some stupid jealous girls."

Sheila walked over and hugged Tashera.

"I love you, Shera, and I'm sorry if I made you worry, but if anyone ever put their hands on you again, I'd do the same thing again. Nobody can change how I believe I should defend you. Nobody."

"Not even a court of law?" Tashera asked.

"I don't think a judge would jail a mom for trying to protect her baby."

"But I'm not a baby anymore," Tashera said.

"You are to me."

Sheila didn't want anyone to tell her that she was wrong for going to Anita Thomas' house. She didn't care if her actions were right or wrong. The most important thing to Sheila was sending a message.

Just as Tashera walked up the stairs, a brick sailed through the living room window. Khalil strolled quickly to the broken window as Sheila walked to the brick and picked it up. The brick had a message taped on it: IT AIN'T OVER.

Chapter 24

It was nearing eight in the evening when Ahmed drove his mother's car to Tashera's neighborhood.

He saw ten-year-old drug pushers outside selling their product to crackheads. A young pregnant girl no more than fourteen performed a lap dance in the middle of the sidewalk for a man old enough to be her grandfather.

He parked in front of Tashera's house and noticed a small board covering an area in the window. He knocked three times on the front door.

Sheila opened the door.

"Good evening, ma'am," Ahmed said.

"Call me Ms. Sheila."

"Okay."

"Tashera, Ahmed is here. You can go on up. Her ribs started to hurt a little, so she's resting in her room."

Ahmed walked through the living room, past a large television with a video game console and controller on the floor in front of it. There was a picture of Khalil and Tashera on top of the TV.

He walked upstairs and saw Tashera lying on her side in a room full of purple: from the rug to the curtains and stuffed animals.

"Hey, Shera," he said.

"Ah-med," Tashera said slowly.

"I really need to talk to you."

Tashera sat up. "I know." Tashera put her trembling hands to her face.

"I called Jessica…"

Tashera cut him off. "What for? People are already saying you been cheating behind my back. Now you're callin' her. What is wrong with you?"

"Tashera, chill, chill for a minute." Ahmed tried to touch Tashera's shoulder, but she yanked herself away.

"When the rumors in school were flying that Jessica had a part in this, I wanted to beat her down," Ahmed began. "No question. But I knew as a guy, it wasn't the thing to do. I'd never get away with it. At the same time, I wanted to do something, so I decided to call her and see if I could get her to confess to everything."

"Confess?" Tashera asked.

"Yes, on my cell phone. I called her to set up a time to go over her house, talk to her, and let her tell me what happened."

"Well, where's the recording?"

"I don't have it."

"Wait a minute. You told me this B.S. story and you don't even have the recording? Get out, Ahmed. I don't think our relationship is going to work. You're obviously not understanding me right now."

"Nah, nah. When I went to see her, two girls in jeans and sweats were talking to her and then they forced her into a car. One of the girls had the number twenty-three etched on her back pocket."

"What are you saying?"

"Mike told me to go to the police, but I didn't know what to say to them. I knew you'd know what to do with the info, so I'm telling you."

"So I can do what? Feel sorry for her?"

"Wait a minute, Tashera. You don't have to go off on me. I want us to be tight like we were before. I figured you'd want to know what was going on."

"I'm sorry, Ahmed. Let's just change the subject."

"What happened to your front window?" Ahmed asked.

"Didn't I just say let's change the subject?"

Ahmed leaned over to Tashera and kissed her on the cheek. "All I want is for you to be happy."

"I don't think I can be happy here," Tashera said and shook her head.

"I know. We need to move. My basketball scholarship ain't comin' fast enough."

"I don't have a basketball scholarship. I'm stuck here."

"As much as I love you, you'll never be stuck."

Tashera turned on the small TV in her bedroom. They laughed at SpongeBob.

"They need to do an episode where Patrick and Spongebob move from Bikini Bottom," Ahmed joked.

"Yeah, and we can try to copy 'em."

Ahmed wanted to hug all of Tashera's pain away. He could see there was so much that she wasn't telling him. The free spirited, innocent girl that he had fallen in love with had become a sad, angry person in a matter of days. He desperately wanted the old Tashera back and wondered if she'd ever reappear.

****

Lady B picked up Khalil and his muzzled dog four blocks down from his house. She chauffeured him over to the abandoned building where he'd kept Jessica hostage for more than a day. He rolled up the ramp, removed Killer's muzzle, and entered the room. The smell of urine smacked him in the face. Jessica laid in a fetal position with her eyes opened.

"Sit up!" Khalil ordered.

Jessica moved as fast as she could and sat on the edge of the bed, facing Khalil. Khalil held the leash tight around Killer's neck as the dog bared his teeth and growled at Jessica.

"Why did you jump my sister?"

Jessica began to cry. Killer continued to growl at her.

"I don't know," Jessica cried.

Khalil loosened the grip on Killer, and the dog inched closer to Jessica, readying to clamp on her ankle.

"I'm 'bout to sic my dog on you."

"We beat her up because of her boyfriend."

Khalil pulled Killer back a little.

"Did Deuce Five put you up to this?" Khalil asked.

"No!" Jessica cried.

"How many times did you hit her?"

Jessica cried harder. Khalil let Killer open his mouth. His cold nose touched Jessica's shin, and she lifted her legs on the bed.

"Ten times," Jessica answered.

"How many times did your crew hit her?"

"Five times."

Khalil loosened his grip. Jessica jumped back. Killer put his paws on the bed and growled.

"It was three of y'all. How many times did the rest of your crew hit my sister?" Khalil stared at Jessica with the coldest eyes.

"Twenty times."

"How many times did you kick her?"

"I didn't kick her."

Khalil pulled back Killer.

"Who kicked her?"

"Calia. Calia was the only one who kicked her."

Khalil and Killer left the room. He locked the door and put the muzzle back on Killer. When Khalil got outside, Lady B was waiting out front.

"B, I want your girls who snatched this ho to come back tomorrow night and beat her, but I only want them to hit her thirty times. They can hit her anywhere, but they can't kick her, they can't use any weapons, just fists. When it's done, I want you to call me."

An eye for an eye, Khalil thought.

Those high school girls didn't know whom they were dealing with when they put their hands on Tashera Odom. They didn't know how her family or the people who loved her would retaliate, but Khalil was determined to show them.

****

Mr. Ryland swam laps at the pool inside his mansion in Potomac, Maryland, after a late-night news broadcast revealed that Jessica Barnes had gone missing.

Mr. Ryland had been swimming a lot lately. He swam the most when he had problems that he couldn't seem to resolve. He'd thought a lot about DeCalia and her mother. He knew DeCalia would be a totally different person if her mother was more caring toward her. As a young basketball player, Mr. Ryland saw plenty of kids' lives turn around because the coaches invested time in them. If parents didn't want to spend time with their kids, the least they could do was enroll them in some kind of sports enrichment program.

Mr. Ryland got out of the pool and toweled himself off. With Jessica missing, he had become increasingly concerned for Alexandra's safety as well. He went into his foyer and called Detective Stewart.

"Stewart," the detective said as he answered the phone.

"Detective, it's Sean Ryland from Marion Barry High."

"What's going on, Mr. Ryland?"

"Remember I told you that I had questioned Alexandra Kent?"

"Yeah."

"Well, my gut tells me that someone should check on her."

"Why do you say that?"

"Well, Jessica is missing, and Alexandra's the other person involved in the fight. Couldn't she be a target?"

"Yeah, but with DeCalia in Oak Hill and Jessica missing, I seriously doubt the same people who took Jessica would risk going after Alexandra right now. There's been too much media out there with Jessica's picture."

"Well, you're the professional. I'll leave it up to you."

"Just keep an eye on her in school. And if anything looks strange to you, give me a call."

"I will. Thanks," Mr. Ryland said and hung up.

To at least feel as if he was helping in some way, Mr. Ryland was determined to keep an eye on Alexandra the best way that he could.

Chapter 25

Detective Stewart hated to deal with work on Saturdays. He'd rather be coaching his son's intramural basketball team, but he couldn't ignore the possibility that Jessica Barnes' disappearance had a direct connection to the attack on Tashera Odom.

He knocked on Sheila Odom's front door.

Sheila opened the door and said, "You must have ESP like the girl on *Medium*. I was just going to call you. You remember that scene in court yesterday? Well, that woman threw a brick through my window last night. It's right over there."

Detective Stewart looked at the brick, then he put on his plastic gloves and put it in a big plastic bag. He always carried his evidence collecting materials wherever he went.

"The same thing that she said to me in court is the same thing she wrote on the brick. Everybody heard her."

"Did you see her outside last night?"

"No, but who else could it be?"

"I don't know. Do you have any enemies?"

"We all have enemies, Stewart—even you."

Tashera walked downstairs and said hello to the detective.

"Tashera, I'm glad you're here. I need to talk to you—to both of you, actually."

132

"Here we go," Sheila said.

"A girl that has been implicated in Tashera's attack has been missing for the past two days. Have you heard anything about that, Tashera?"

Tashera looked at the ground and then stared at the picture of her and Khalil above the television.

"Nah," she said, "I've been outta the loop since I've been in the hospital."

"Have you talked with anyone from school since you've been home?"

"Um—just Ahmed."

"That's your boyfriend, right?"

"Yeah."

"He didn't tell you about that?"

"Why would he?"

"A lot of rumors circulate in school. Mrs. Odom, have you heard anything from the other parents at school or your neighbors?"

"Do I look like I'm a member of the PTA? I just got out of jail yesterday. The only people that I've talked to are my kids."

"Where's Khalil?"

"He's a grown man. I don't know where he is."

"Doesn't he still live here?"

"Yes. Just 'cause he ain't here and you're here doesn't mean he moved," Sheila said.

"I need him to call me when he gets back." Detective Stewart pulled a card from his pocket and handed it to Sheila before walking out the front door.

He noticed that Tashera didn't give him any eye contact when he asked her about Jessica. And when he asked her about Ahmed, she started to ball her fist and release it. Detective Stewart sat in his car and sifted through papers full of phone numbers that he'd put in the glove box. He retrieved a piece of notebook paper that contained Ahmed's name and number. Tashera had given it to him the first time that he'd met her.

If anyone knew what Tashera was holding back on, it was probably Ahmed.

****

Khalil wheeled himself through the front door and stopped in his bedroom before heading to the bathroom to wash up. He'd spent the night over his friend Fitz's house.

When he finished showering and returned to his room, he found Tashera sitting on his bed.

"Hey, li'l sis," he said. "What's the good wit' ya?"

The police came here today about Jessica."

Khalil thought about saying, "Who is Jessica?" but there was no point to that. His sister knew when he was lying or trying to cover up something.

"What happened?" Khalil asked.

"Detective Stewart was here asking if me or Mom knew anything about it."

"It's all under control. Don't worry 'bout that. It'll be over soon." Khalil started brushing his hair.

"No, it won't. What if there are witnesses?"

Khalil put down his brush and looked Tashera straight in the eye. Anger had begun to crawl up his spine.

"Are you telling me that someone saw something?" he asked.

"No," Tashera said quickly.

"Then what are you saying?"

"I'm not saying anything," Tashera said and walked out of Khalil's room.

Tashera wouldn't have mentioned witnesses if there were none, Khalil thought. *The only person she talks to is Ahmed. I need to track him down.*

Khalil finished dressing and went to Fitz's house. He had to come up with a strategy to talk with Ahmed without his sister finding out.

****

Alexandra sat at the kitchen table and watched the news reports about Jessica's disappearance. She desperately wanted to talk to DeCalia who always knew how to respond in stressful situations. Alexandra called DeCalia's cell phone, hoping police had released her, but it went straight to voicemail. She immediately tried DeCalia's house phone.

"Hello," Fran said.

"Is DeCalia there?" Alexandra asked.

"No, who is this?"

"Alex, I'm one of her friends from school."

"She's in Oak Hill," Fran said.

"The jail for kids?"

"Yeah. You won't see her in school for a while."

"Thanks for telling me. We were really close."

Alexandra stared at the phone and thought about calling her mom. Her mother was a researcher for a powerful lobbyist firm in DC. Her mother wrote reports on why tobacco companies should be able to advertise cigarette smoking on billboards around playgrounds, schools, arcades, and youth centers. Her mother was always busy, flying out of town, attending political events, "protecting her clients' rights," she'd always say.

"It seems weird that you could work for a company that is paid to help another company give people cancer," Alexandra told her mother earlier in the year.

"It's not about cancer," her mother said. "It's about the freedom of advertisement and free enterprise."

Alexandra pulled out a pack of Newports and a new lighter that she had purchased specifically for this conversation. She ripped the pack open, put the cigarette in her mouth, and began to put the flame to the tip of the cigarette.

"What do you think you're doing?" her mother asked.

"Since it's not about cancer, I've decided to start smoking. I'll make sure I blow enough smoke for the both of us."

Her mother snatched the cigarette out of her mouth and took the pack and threw them in the trash.

"You're so smart, Alexandra. If you put that kind of thought into your schoolwork, you'd be a straight-A student."

Alexandra had lost all respect for her mother when she learned about her job. She couldn't believe her mother could put making money over all the people who were dying and would eventually die because of smoking.

To further make a point to her mother, Alexandra started smoking anyway and had developed at least a two-pack-a-week habit.

Alexandra went into her bedroom where she looked at a heart-shaped frame with a picture of her and her dad inside. Her mother and father divorced at the end of her eighth grade year. Her father moved to Atlanta and within a year, had found a new person to marry and had already started a family.

When her father first moved, he called Alexandra every day to get an update on how she was doing. When she started the ninth grade, he reduced his calls to three times a week. By the end of ninth grade, she talked to her father once a week and now, two years later, she only spoke to him during holidays. If her mother ever remarried, she'd probably never speak to her father again. She couldn't call her father and talk to him about her problems.

Alexandra went to the bathroom, reached under the cabinet, and pulled out some old hair clippers. She plugged the clippers into the wall socket. She stared at herself in the mirror. Her shoulder-length hair was pulled into a messy bun. She'd developed bags under her eyes from not being able to sleep. Her skin had gotten blotchy from all the worrying she'd done for the past couple of days.

Alexandra turned on the clippers and placed them at the front of her head. She shaved one strip closest to her right ear. Then she shaved a second strip closest to her left ear. Within a few seconds, all of Alexandra's hair was on the floor. Alexandra left the clippers on the counter and the hair on the floor. She went to her room and lay on the bed in a tight ball.

Chapter 26

Richard King drove through his old neighborhood in Southeast. Nothing looked as good as it looked thirty years ago. He didn't remember seeing as many disheveled looking people as he did today. The streets were cleaner then—there wasn't the number of broken bottles or debris lying around. The people looked different—somehow they were happier, less afraid than they were now.

Richard pulled up to Sheila's house. She had called him after Detective Stewart dropped by her house.

Sheila had seen Richard drive up in his spotless Mercedes Benz truck and was waiting for him at the door when he walked up.

"Nice ride," she said. "You came down here showing off."

"I get more tax write-offs from driving a Benz than from driving a Honda, but that's not why I'm here," Richard said, "so let's stick to the issues."

People who tried to size him up by the type of car that he drove annoyed Richard beyond belief. He could afford his Mercedes Benz, and because he was a business owner, the luxury car's depreciation saved him thousands of dollars in taxes—a concept he wished more African Americans understood. Most of his childhood friends that drove luxury cars had cars that cost more than their homes and were one paycheck away from either getting kicked out of their homes or having their car repossessed.

Once they were seated in the living room, Sheila said, "I had a brick thrown through my window last night. I think Anita did it."

"Where's the brick?" Richard asked.

"The detective took it."

"You hadn't called the detective to report the brick, right?"

"No."

"Well, why was he here in the first place?"

"He told us that one of the girls who attacked Tashera is missing."

Richard sighed. "I saw that on the news this morning."

"What goes around, comes around," Sheila said.

Richard looked at Sheila and shook his head.

"She's still a seventeen-year-old girl."

"Nobody was thinking that when they attacked Tashera," Sheila said.

"There is too much violence and hate in this area."

"Well, I'm not running away like you did."

Richard chuckled.

"You're the same old Sheila. You will always be limited to your own worldview. Forget about widening the lens, huh? I didn't run away and neither did my parents. We moved to an area where there were more opportunities for me. I could go to school and be expected to learn, not expected to fail. Don't you want that for Tashera?"

"People are always talking about the DC school system, but there are some good teachers in that system."

"Of course there are, but what about the violence? Look at what happened to Tashera. Look at what happened to Khalil. He's in a wheelchair for Christ's sakes. If you lived somewhere else, do you believe these things would have happened?"

"Maybe they would have. I'm not running away from anything," Sheila said.

"Maybe it's time you started to think about running *to* something—a better way of life, for example."

"What are you gonna do about the brick through my window?" Sheila asked and rolled her eyes.

"I'm going to call the Detective, try to see if he's going to get handwriting analysis, interrogate Anita, that sort of thing. I'm also going to try to get an emergency hearing on Monday to get the charges dropped and a restraining order put in place. The more this woman attempts to attack or antagonize you, the more she looks like the perpetrator instead of the victim."

Sheila nodded.

Richard leaned forward on the sofa and stretched out his hands, as if pleading to someone. "I have one last question for you," he said.

Sheila groaned. "What?"

"If you didn't live in Southeast, do you think you'd be having this situation with Anita? Do you think when you went to her house, it would have led to a physical altercation? Do you think she'd throw a brick through your window?"

"That ain't one question."

"But it's something to think about."

Richard knew there was no escaping violence, but there were certainly areas that had more incidents of violence than others. There were areas in which the school systems were better. The children of Southeast DC weren't to blame for the violence that surrounded their community, but somebody was to blame. And until anyone could figure out how to resolve the violence crisis, Richard wasn't sure if DC was a good enough place to raise a family.

Once out in his truck, Richard called his office and left himself a voice mail, "Call Detective Stewart regarding the Anita Thomas investigation and brick. Email and call the judge regarding new threats of violence against Sheila Odom."

Did the violence ever stop in DC? Richard thought. *Did anyone ever believe in walking away?*

****

When DeCalia woke up, she was sadder than she had ever been. Though she had dreamed she was back at home with her mom, reality set in and she was still a detainee in Oak Hill. They had placed her in a room that resembled a cell from HBO's prison show *Oz*, and the mattress was thinner than a yoga mat. Last night as she tried to sleep, DeCalia swore she heard rodents crawling in her room and in the hallway. She had to wear some facility issued itchy sweat pants and a rough t-shirt to bed. She'd given her left arm to be able to walk to the laundry mat with her mom or Fran to wash her own clothes in some real detergent.

DeCalia laid her head back on the floppy mattress. She wasn't ready to get up anyway. The sounds of the other teens walking back and forth awakened her.

"Breakfast," DeCalia heard one of the guards yell.

She sat up and looked underneath the bed for her sneakers. They were gone. The multi-colored DC's were her favorite kicks. She had even graffitied a small *dc* on the side with her neon pen.

Maybe someone took the shoes when I took a shower last night, she thought. *Would the guards be so crabby as to steal from one of the kids?*

DeCalia slid her feet into her Oak Hill issued shower shoes and walked into the dining area. She went through the line and was served some yellow mush that was supposed to be eggs, gray pebbles that were supposed to oatmeal, and a piece of cardboard with a yellow pat of glue on top of it that was supposed to be toast. She looked for a place to sit and tried to find a friendly face among the sea of hardened grills. She didn't find any, so she sat by herself at the end of a table. Within a few minutes, another girl that DeCalia remembered from their bus ride over to Oak Hill sat across from her. The girl didn't say anything and DeCalia just stared at her food—she wasn't hungry enough to eat food that looked so disgusting.

DeCalia observed the girls who left the line. Many of them were wearing sweatpants and t-shirts that were identical to hers. Some of them were wearing ugly black sneakers with Velcro like they were still learning how to tie shoelaces. DeCalia shook her head and then she spotted a girl about her height who'd walked out of the food line with her DC's on.

"She got my shoes," DeCalia said. "That ain't gonna fly."

DeCalia walked over to one of the guards from yesterday.

"Guard. That girl over there has my shoes."

"What do you want me to do about it?" The guard asked.

"Don't you have a rule about people stealing other people's property?"

"How do we know those are your shoes?"

"I had them on yesterday when you strip searched me."

"I don't remember that. I don't think they're your shoes," the guard said.

DeCalia almost felt tears coming to her eyes. She shook her head. She refused to cry twice in two days, but she was going to find a way to get her shoes back.

"Why don't you go ask her where she got those shoes from?" she asked.

"Why don't you ask her?" The guard said.

"Okay, I will." DeCalia marched over to the girl who'd been talking and eating with a bunch of other girls.

"Those are my shoes," DeCalia said. "Take them off."

"My mom sent me these shoes," the girl said, throwing her hand in DeCalia's direction. "You better get outta my face."

"How'd your mom send you a pair of shoes that I already wrote on? She must be a thief just like you, skank."

The girl got up and lunged at DeCalia. The guard grabbed DeCalia and restrained her and the other girl was able to hit DeCalia a couple of times in the stomach. DeCalia doubled over in pain.

The guard kneeled over. "Do you still want your sneakers, Dummy?"

DeCalia's eyes turned red. Never in her life had anyone taken anything from her and gotten away with it. She walked back into her room and started to think about a strategy to get her shoes back.

****

Detective Stewart sat in the kitchen of the Barnes' residence with Jessica's mother, Lenise.

"Is there anything you can tell me about Jessica's disposition the last couple of days?" he asked.

Lenise rested her hands on the table. "She seemed real happy one day and her friends seemed to be ringing the phone off the hook," she said. "Lately, whenever I would come in the room, she would start whispering."

"Whispering?"

"Yeah and I found that strange because we talked about everything. She even asked me a couple of weeks ago how to get back at some guy who betrayed her."

"Really. What did you tell her?"

"Nothing really. Just that men are sensitive about the things that they're close to, anything where their hearts are involved."

"Like a new girlfriend," Detective Stewart said.

"Exactly."

"Where is Jessica's cell phone?"

"It's still in her room, on the charger."

"Do you have the code to her voice mail?"

"Yes. That's how close we are."

"Please go get the phone."

When Lenise returned with the phone, Detective Stewart said, "Call voice mail, enter the code, and then hand me the phone."

Detective Stewart listened to several messages, but one stood out in particular: *It's Ahmed. If it's true that you had something to do with what happened, you're gonna pay. Make no mistake, you're gonna pay.*

"I need to take this cell phone in for evidence," Detective Stewart said. "I'll get it back to you as soon as I can."

"I don't care. If you think it'll help you find Jessica, you can have the phone."

Ahmed threatened Jessica a couple of days before she disappeared, Detective Stewart thought as he walked to his car. *That is definitely probable cause.*

****

Ahmed and the basketball team ran lay ups in the gym. When the coach blew the whistle for a fifteen-minute break, Mike came over.

"Yo Ahmed," he said, "that was a sweet lay up pass that you threw to Rafael."

Ahmed just nodded. He wasn't trying to talk to Mike. He was still pissed at how Mike treated him because of what he saw happening to Jessica.

"You hook up with Tashera yet?"

"Man, don't worry about that. I'm chillin'," Ahmed said.

"Oh, it's like that. You don't have any words for me now."

"I don't got time," Ahmed said and started to walk away.

"We can knuckle up right here if you gotta problem wit' me," Mike yelled.

Ahmed had Mike by about three inches and at least fifteen pounds. Ahmed was the star of the team; Mike warmed the bench. Ahmed knew that if he put one hand on Mike, he could get suspended from the team and possibly jeopardize his scholarships. Mike wouldn't lose anything except a few teeth that could be replaced.

A couple of other team members started to circle around Ahmed and Mike.

"Punch him into next week, Ahmed," one of the teammates yelled.

"Punch a hole threw him," another teammate called out.

"When there's some real competition, let me know," Ahmed said and walked away with the team following at his heel.

"You're a punk, Ahmed," Mike said. "In every possible way."

****

Detective Stewart had entered the gym while Ahmed and Mike were yelling at each other. After the fiasco was over, he introduced himself to the coach, told him he'd spoken with Ahmed's mom and that he needed to speak with Ahmed for a few minutes.

"Ahmed," Coach said.

"I didn't do anything," Ahmed said.

"Come here, boy. I didn't ask for any explanation."

Ahmed walked to Coach.

"This is Detective Stewart. He just came from your house. Your mom said it was okay to speak with you. Talk with him. Help him if you can. You understand?"

"Yes sir."

"Where do you wanna talk?" Detective Stewart asked.

"Outside."

Detective Stewart and Ahmed walked to the outdoor basketball court with Ahmed bouncing a basketball along the way.

"Did you see Tashera yesterday?" Detective Stewart asked.

Ahmed stopped dribbling the ball and gave all of his attention to Stewart. "Did something happen to her? Is she okay?"

"Calm down, calm down. She's fine. I'm just gonna ask you some questions."

"Yeah," Ahmed replied as he began dribbling again. "I saw her yesterday."

"What did you two talk about?"

Ahmed shrugged. "Nothing really."

"Nothing? Give me an idea."

"We talked about SpongeBob."

"Anything else?"

"We talked about movin'."

"Moving? You are a little young to be thinking about that, aren't you?"

"Am I? I'm a senior this year. I'll be leaving for college in two months."

"You going into a summer program?"

"Yeah."

"Do you know Jessica Barnes?"

"Yeah."

"How?"

"I used to date her."

"When did you stop dating her?"

"Last summer. Why are you asking me these questions about Jessica?"

"Haven't you seen the news? She is missing."

Detective Stewart stared hard at Ahmed. Ahmed didn't blink. He didn't stop dribbling. He didn't seem surprised about Jessica's disappearance.

"That's jacked up," Ahmed said.

"Jacked up? That's all you can say? She could be dead in an alley somewhere and all you can say is that's jacked up?"

"What do you want me to say? She was a stupid winch and she probably got what was coming to her."

"Are you saying that because you had a hand in what happened to her?"

"No."

"Take me to your locker," Detective Stewart said.

Ahmed groaned and marched back into the school. At his locker, he pointed and said, "There it is."

"Where's your cell phone?"

Ahmed dug in the front of his backpack and pulled out his cell phone.

Detective Stewart pulled out a piece of paper that had Jessica's cell phone number on it and then he looked at the cell phone call history on Ahmed's cell phone.

"Two days ago, the same day that Jessica was kidnapped, you made several calls to her cell phone. Think that's a coincidence?"

"I just called her to talk about what happened to Tashera. I wanted to get her to confess."

"I don't think so. I think you set her up. Put your hands behind your back," Detective Stewart said and pulled out his handcuffs. "You're under arrest for kidnapping Jessica Barnes." He placed the cuffs on Ahmed.

"I didn't have anything to do with that," Ahmed yelled. "COO-ACH!"

Coach raced into the locker room. Ahmed turned to him and said, "Call my mom. They're arresting me."

Coach came over to Detective Stewart.

"I'm sure this is a mistake," he said.

"It's no mistake," Detective Stewart said. "I'm sorry."

Detective Stewart led Ahmed out of the gym by his elbow.

.

Chapter 27

Jessica hadn't eaten in two days. As she lay on the bed in soiled clothing, she thought about her mother--the Mother's Days that she wouldn't get to spend with her, the holidays that would come and go and she wouldn't be around her family.

Jessica remembered that she once had a dream of being homecoming queen at Howard University. She had planned to apply to college this year and get accepted. She had even planned to get a scholarship by pushing herself and working her tail off. But where had those dreams gone?

Jessica knew that the human body could go several days without food and water, but she felt her heart had begun to beat more and more slowly. Her will to keep breathing seemed to pass with every waking minute.

As Jessica fell asleep again, she heard two female voices coming up the hallway.

"Help," Jessica said weakly, hoping that the two women were the police or paramedics that had sensed she was in danger.

Instead of the door being kicked in as in a life-saving emergency, Jessica listened as someone jiggled a key into the lock on the other side. Jessica closed her eyes and pretended to be dead.

"Is she dead already?" one girl asked.

One girl put her finger underneath Jessica's nose. "No the heifer is still in the land of the living. She just passed out or something."

"I got something for that."

The girl took her water bottle and poured it over Jessica's face. Jessica shook her head and started to gag. Some of the water had gone up her nostrils.

"See, she's alive."

Jessica looked at the two girls. She couldn't be sure, but they reminded her of the two girls who kidnapped her from her house. Jessica wanted to lift up her head, but she didn't have the strength.

"Help me," Jessica said.

"Help you?" one girl asked, then they both laughed.

"We're here to hurt you."

One girl grabbed Jessica by the shoulder and sat her up, then the other girl punched her in her jaw. One girl punched Jessica in the stomach, then the other girl punched her in the back of the head. They took turns hitting Jessica and counted each lick from one through thirty. Jessica couldn't hear any counting or other noise after she heard the number eleven. She'd passed out.

The two girls carried Jessica's body and put it in the trunk of their car then they drove away.

****

Tashera had called Ahmed's cell phone several times. He was scheduled to be done with basketball practice around one o'clock. She called him again and left a message.

"Ahmed, call me when you get this. I want to go to the mall today. I need a change of atmosphere. My mom is buggin' right now. I need to see you. I need to get away."

Since Ahmed hadn't called her back, she decided to call Mike to see if he knew what was up with Ahmed.

"Hello," Mike said.

"Hey Mike. This is Tashera. Is Ahmed wit' you?"

"Not hardly."

"Oh. Um. My fault. I thought y'all were rollin' together after basketball practice."

"Nah. Five-O came and got your boy."

"What?"

"The police came and picked him up in the middle of practice. Coach was here. Everybody saw it."

"Thanks for telling me, Mike."

Tashera's heart raced. She couldn't think of one reason that Ahmed would be in custody. Tashera thought of all the things Ahmed had told her about the girl Jessica and still couldn't think of anything that would make the police think he was guilty of anything.

She had to find a way to get to the police station to be there for Ahmed.

Tashera called Ahmed's home phone.

"Hello?"

"Mrs. Warner, it's Tashera. I wanted to know if you were on your way to see Ahmed?"

"I'm on my way out the door."

"I would love to come with you."

"I'm on my way."

Tashera went to the kitchen and saw her mother washing dishes.

"I'm going to see Ahmed," she said, barely getting every word out. "He's in jail. I'm going to ride over with his mother."

Sheila spun around and faced Tashera. "Is this over what happened to you?" she asked.

Tashera forced herself to keep her tears in check. She nodded.

Sheila wrapped her arms around Tashera and pulled her into a hug. "Be careful," she whispered as she kissed the top of Tashera's head.

Tashera turned and raced from the house. *Everything has to be okay with Ahmed*, she thought. *He's the rock that's holding me together.*

****

During free time, DeCalia went outside with the rest of the girls. Some of them played basketball, some played cards, and some even showcased their double dutch skills. No matter how normal it seemed while DeCalia walked around outside, the sight of the barbed wire fencing reminded her that she was a prisoner. When she spotted the girl who'd had breakfast with her earlier that day, she went over to her.

"Hey. My name's DeCalia."

"I'm Renee. It's too bad about your shoes. Nettie always does stuff like that to newcomers."

"I look new?" DeCalia asked.

"Yeah and scared to death."

DeCalia couldn't believe somebody—a girl who looked like she could be the newest addition to the Bratz doll collection no less—told her that she looked scared.

"What are you here for anyway?" Renee asked.

"Fighting," DeCalia said. "I thought you were new, too. I remembered seeing you on the bus."

"This is my third time in here."

"What you in here for?"

"Prostitution."

DeCalia had to tighten her face to prevent her jaw from dropping. Renee didn't look much older than thirteen and already she'd been turning tricks and had done enough that she'd been caught.

"You want to get Nettie back and get your shoes back at the same time?"

"Yeah."

"Be like the first person to be in the shower line and we'll hook up afterwards."

"I'll be there," DeCalia said. She didn't know what Renee had in store, but every time she saw Nettie walking around in her DC's, she wanted to chop her feet off.

****

Khalil sat in Lady B's apartment in Stanton Glenn. Boxes surrounded the couch.

"You're really leavin', huh?" he asked.

"There's nothing for me here," Lady B replied.

"What about the crew?"

"The crew?" Lady B laughed. "Since Darren got knocked, you think people from the crew been coming by to make sure I'm straight? You think people checkin' for him in Ohio? Nobody does anything for us."

"Dang. I didn't know it was like that."

"That crew loyalty is a lie if you're in a crew with a bunch of yellow bellies. Everybody is tough until they get knocked or catch a case."

Khalil thought about how he'd been treated since his paralysis. His treatment wasn't the same and he knew it, but he believed the gang was down for whatever.

"It's time to go," Lady B said.

They got on the elevator and exited the building.

Lady B drove to a vacant lot as Khalil had instructed her. After about ten minutes, the girls who had Jessica in their trunk arrived and stood near the trunk.

Khalil got out of the car and went to the back of the trunk. One of the girls popped the trunk.

Khalil looked at Jessica. Her face was swollen and bloodied. *Tashera didn't look as bad her first day in the hospital,* he thought. *But Tashera was innocent. This girl was not.*

"Set her down over there," Khalil said.

"In the open?" One of the girls asked.

Khalil nodded.

The two girls took Jessica's limp body and lay it on open pavement. They hopped in their car and left.

Khalil got back into Lady B's car.

"When you gonna be really out of the area?" Khalil asked.

"Two or three days. Maybe sooner. Now that this is done, what's next for you?"

"We got a brick through my mom's front window."

"From who?"

"One of the parents of the girls who attacked my sister. My moms went over to her house and beat her down."

"What is going on?"

"She calls herself retaliatin', but she don't know the half."

"Some mess you need to let go of or you'll be fighting this battle forever."

"It is what it is," Khalil said. "I don't see you letting a brick come through your crib unanswered."

"It depends. Gettin' caught can really stop your shine—stop you from doin' you wit' ya life."

"B, you have changed a lot. I'm glad to see you makin' moves, but never forget where you came from."

"How could I? I know you'll always be somewhere reminding me," Lady B said and got the wheelchair out of the car for Khalil. She put down the wheel lock and Khalil positioned himself on the seat out front of his house.

Lady B was right. He'd never let her forget who she was. The only way she'd be able to start over is if she left the old neighborhood and the people from it.

Chapter 28

Ahmed's mother and Tashera entered the 7th District Metropolitan Police Department and went straight to the front desk.

"I'm here to see my son Ahmed Warner," Mrs. Warner said. "He was on his way here about an hour ago. He's a minor."

"Have a seat. I'll find out where he is and let you know," the desk sergeant said.

Mrs. Warner and Tashera sat next to each other. Tashera shook her right leg impatiently.

"Calm down, Tashera. It'll be okay," Mrs. Warner said and patted Tashera's knee.

Tashera started to shake her head.

"I know this is somehow my fault," she muttered.

"We don't even know what he's in here for yet, so we gotta stay calm until we get the facts."

"I can't be calm. Too much has happened this week." Tashera cried and walked away from Mrs. Warner.

Mrs. Warner walked over to her. "It doesn't seem like it was a good idea for you to come. This is upsetting you. Why don't you call your mother to come pick you up? Me and Ahmed will be okay."

"No," Tashera said and wiped her face. "I'll be okay. I want to be here for Ahmed."

"Hello Tashera," Detective Stewart said as he walked toward them. "Mrs. Warner, I'm Detective Stewart. I can take you back to see Ahmed. Is Tashera coming with us?"

"Yes. Do you know why he's here? " Mrs. Warner said.

"Yes, I arrested him for kidnapping."

"What?" Mrs. Warner asked.

"A girl that he used to date is missing."

Tashera felt her legs get wobbly. The police had arrested Ahmed for Khalil's deeds. Deuce Trés had put Ahmed, his scholarship, and his future in jeopardy for something that he didn't do.

I love my brother, Tashera thought, *but I don't know if I can sacrifice Ahmed's freedom for my family.*

****

DeCalia was the first to get to the shower area. After she dried off and put her clothes back on, she looked around for Renee. Renee had told her to meet her in the side hallway by the kitchen. Most of the guards supervised the girls in the shower, so they would be able to talk about getting her shoes back. When she got close to the kitchen, she didn't see Renee, but she felt some eyes staring at her. She turned around and saw Nettie and three of her friends walking behind her.

"I hear you still want your shoes," Nettie said, punching her hand in her fist.

DeCalia looked around. *Where was Renee?* she thought. How was she gonna fight off four girls by herself? As the four girls circled her just as she and her friends had circled Tashera, DeCalia realized that Renee wasn't coming to meet her. Renee had set the whole thing up.

Nettie took the first swing at DeCalia's head, but DeCalia swerved and threw a tight fist into Nettie's rib. It must have hit a soft spot because Nettie bent over to her side. DeCalia felt a force from behind hit her squarely on her ear. It caused her to lose balance, and she fell forward and latched on to the bottom of Nettie's legs, causing her to hit the ground, too. DeCalia could feel blows being rained down all over her body. But no matter how much pain she felt, she didn't let go of Nettie's ankles. Her shoes were attached to Nettie's ankles.

A whistle sounded off from the shower area.

"We gotta go," one of the girls said.

"She won't let go of my feet," Nettie said. "Pull her off of me."

The girls tried to pull DeCalia off of Nettie, but DeCalia was heavier than the other girls and she had latched on to Nettie like a padlock.

The girls started to run to the shower. Nettie started wiggling her legs and feet. The shoes came off and she got up and kept running to the shower.

DeCalia just lay there with her arms circled around her DC's. She cried a full body cry.

DeCalia sat up, put on her sneakers, and wiped the wetness from her face. She didn't want to be in a place where girls fought each other over other people's property. She didn't want to be in a place where the people in authority didn't protect the kids. She didn't want to be in a place where she could get set up for absolutely no reason. As DeCalia walked back to her cell, she'd thought about the attack on Tashera—the single act that got her here.

****

Alexandra called her mother's cell phone, but her mother didn't pick up.

She left a message: "Mom, I really need to speak with you. Please call home and come as soon as you can."

Alexandra hadn't talked to her friends in what seemed like a lifetime. She had begun to bite her nails again; she'd even gone searching in the liquor cabinet to numb her pain, but she had found no alcohol. Alexandra had forgotten that after her mother started seeing a shrink last year, she declared their household alcohol free. Apparently, when her mother felt stressed she drank, and the psychiatrist told her to get rid of the alcohol. And then the psychiatrist prescribed her mother a little pill to make her feel better when she felt overstressed. Alexandra continued her search—this time for the little pills. Maybe they'd help release her stress also.

****

Anita Thomas sat on the couch and drank a beer. She heard a knock on her front door. She opened the door and saw Detective Rodriguez on the other side.

"What do you want?" Anita asked.

"To talk to you for a minute."

Anita opened the door wider and motioned for Detective Rodriguez to enter. Anita headed back toward the couch. Detective Rodriguez followed and saw that the glass and shards from the broken table were still lying on the floor.

"You not worried about your son getting cut from all of this broken glass?" Detective Rodriguez asked.

"He'll be alright."

"What about you? You're sitting in the middle of it almost daring it to cut you."

"You didn't come here to talk about glass, so get to your point or get out."

"Have you tried to talk to DeCalia since she's been in Oak Hill?"

"No"

"Why not?"

"I've been busy."

"Have you ever been inside a juvenile detention facility?"

"No."

"It's a place where some bad kids and not-so-bad kids who've made mistakes are all thrown in together. When they first get there, there's a big difference between the bad kids and the not-so-bad kids. But after a couple of weeks, the not-so-bad kids start to give up. They stop believing that anybody cares about them. They become as angry and hate-filled as the bad kids."

Detective Rodriguez continued to talk about parents and their responsibilities while Anita chain-smoked and stared at the television.

****

Mrs. Warner and Tashera sat on the same side of the table, and Detective Stewart sat at the end. Two police officers escorted Ahmed inside. Mrs. Warner and Tashera jumped up and approached him. He hugged his mother first then Tashera.

"Ahmed, why don't you tell your mother what is going on," Detective Stewart said.

"Mom, I didn't do anything."

"Who is the girl that they're saying was kidnapped?" Mrs. Warner asked.

"Jessica. Remember the girl from last summer?"

"Oh my God. I told you she was bad news, but you didn't believe me. You had to find out the hard way."

"Mom, I didn't do anything to Jessica."

"Detective, what are you alleging here?"

"We have a threat on her cell phone from Ahmed—a threat is probable cause."

"Why did you threaten her?"

"Because she and her friends jumped Tashera."

Mrs. Warner looked at Tashera.

"I just threatened her," Ahmed said. "I didn't hit her or anything."

"Why'd you keep calling her?" Detective Stewart asked.

"Because I came up with the idea to get her to confess to what she'd done. I called her to set up a time to meet with her. I was planning to go over to her house with my tape recorder and ask her questions."

"And she was just gonna tell you, huh?" Detective Stewart asked.

"If she thought I liked her again, she would have told me."

"What happened when you met up with her?"

"I didn't meet up with her."

"Why not?"

"She wasn't home."

"You expect me to believe that?"

"It's the truth."

Just then Detective Stewart's cell phone rang. He stepped away from the room and answered his phone.

"Is this Detective Stewart?"

"Yeah. Who is this?"

"Don't worry 'bout who it is. I got some information on Ahmed Warner."

"What is it?"

"I can't tell you over the phone. We need to meet."

"Where?"

"Out front of the new shopping area on the corner of Alabama and Stanton. Give me an hour."

The caller hung up, and Detective Stewart returned to the interrogation room.

"Mrs. Warner," he said, "we have to keep Ahmed overnight. If anything new develops, I'll let you know."

Ahmed got up and Tashera hugged him tight. His mother went over and kissed him on the cheek.

"We'll see you tomorrow," Mrs. Warner said.

Everything about Ahmed's body language said that he was telling the truth about Jessica, but there still seemed to be something lurking underneath. Maybe the person who called Detective Stewart's phone would help him find out what it was.

****

Detective Stewart sat in his car and drank a diet cola. Everything that had gone on in the past week at Marion High was unfortunate. It was like a community had gone wild, he thought. An hour had passed while he'd waited for the person who'd called to show up. After an hour and a half, Detective Warner decided to leave.

"The kid probably didn't want to turn in his best friend," Detective Stewart mumbled to himself. "Only thing I have to do is find out who is Ahmed Warner's best friend."

Chapter 29

Sunday, April 8
Six days after the attack

Jessica lay with her face down on the black asphalt. She felt the small rocks and particles against her skin. She tried to open both her eyes, but the right one felt heavy and would not open at all. She squinted because of all the sunlight that had hit her left eye. She tasted blood in her mouth.

"Help me," she said in a barely audible tone. Jessica lifted her right arm in the air, and it seemed to weigh two hundred pounds. She dropped her arm back down to the ground and passed out.

****

Ashe's Sunday mornings with his grandmother started early today. He decided to do a forty-minute jog around the neighborhood to get his blood pumping. Running helped him clear his head and get him to appreciate everything that had gone on in his life. Lately, though, Ashe didn't quite understand why he was put in such close proximity of the person he most hated when he was in high school. Ashe had memories of Khalil and his crew beating up kids in the bathroom and taking their lunch money and gold chains. One time a boy told Ashe that Khalil and his crew took his new Air Jordans.

What does a crew do with one pair of Jordans? Ashe thought. *Pass 'em around and take turns wearing them?*

Ashe hated Khalil and his gang, but Khalil mostly. He hated Khalil more because he was the ringleader and at any time he could have decided to be less violent, less intimidating, less hurtful to everybody else who went to Marion Barry. But he never seemed to care about that. Khalil always brought the worse, most negative possibilities to every situation that he entered. Ashe had never forgotten that.

Ashe turned the corner and prepared to cut through the vacant lot and make a diagonal beeline to his grandmother's backdoor when he saw what appeared to be a female figure lying lifeless on the ground. Ashe sped up and bent over to her. From the pictures that had been posted on telephone poles in the neighborhood and the couple of news stories on television, Ashe believed the girl that lay on the ground was Jessica Barnes.

Ashe felt for a pulse. *Weak*, he thought. *But at least there is one.* He pulled out his cell phone and requested an ambulance to come pick up Jessica.

"Wake up, Jessica. My name is Ashe. I'm a paramedic. We're going to get you to the hospital soon."

Jessica let out a moan.

Ashe looked around the vacant lot. Jessica had been left in almost the exact spot where he'd found Tashera. *Somebody was trying to send the girls who attacked Tashera a message*, Ashe thought. *I bet real money that it's Khalil.* Ashe felt the taste in his mouth sour. His hatred for Khalil grew a little more.

****

Last night, Alexandra had found the anti-anxiety and anti-depressant pills in her mother's medicine cabinet. She'd poured ten pills from each bottle in her hand. As she had contemplated taking them, the house phone rang.

"Hello."

"Alex, I got your message," her mother said. "Is everything okay?"

"Not really. A lot of things are going bad with my friends."

"I'll try to cut this meeting short and get to you tonight. I promise I'll be there for you tonight."

Alexandra smiled at the thought that her mother would come to her rescue. She placed the pills on her nightstand and anxiously waited for her mother to come home. She was excited that they could possibly have a real conversation. Alexandra so wanted to tell somebody what had gone on with her, DeCalia, and Jessica.

Alexandra started to get drowsy, so she went downstairs and lay on the couch. She knew she'd wake up when her mother opened the door.

This morning, though, when Alexandra woke around eight a.m., her mother still had not come home.

Her mother broke her promise, and though normally a broken promise by her mother would not be devastating, this morning, it broke something inside of Alexandra.

She went up to her room and turned on the television. She looked at her call history on her cell phone. Her mother hadn't bothered to try to reach her on her cell phone, and none of her friends had called. Alexandra took the picture of her and her father and put it in her top dresser drawer. She went over to her desk and grabbed a black magic marker. She wrote NOBODY'S GONNA SAVE ME on her mirror.

Alexandra went back over to her desk and pulled out two sheets of paper. On the top of one piece of paper, she wrote *Dad* and on the other piece of paper, she wrote *Mom*.

DAD,

I COULDN'T BE HAPPY FOR YOU BEFORE WHEN YOU TOLD ME ABOUT MY LITTLE BROTHER ADAM. I COULDN'T BE HAPPY BECAUSE I FELT THAT HE WAS GETTING ALL THE TIME FROM YOU THAT I SHOULD HAVE BEEN GETTING. YOU PROBABLY DON'T REMEMBER THIS, BUT WE USED TO DO LOTS OF THINGS TOGETHER—RIDE BIKES, GO SWIMMING, GO TO THE GROCERY STORE. EVER SINCE YOU AND MOM BROKE UP, YOU DON'T HARDLY CALL ME AT ALL. YOU DON'T CHECK UP ON ME. YOU DON'T DO ANY OF THE THINGS THAT YOU USED TO DO. BUT I GUESS IT'S KINDA HARD TO BE A FATHER IN TWO FAMILIES. WELL, NOW, YOU DON'T HAVE TO. GOOD LUCK WITH ADAM. NOW, HERE'S SOME ADVICE FOR YOU-IF YOU AND YOUR WIFE, YOU KNOW, WHAT'S HER NAME, EVER SEPARATE, DON'T TAKE IT OUT ON ADAM. HE DIDN'T DO ANYTHING. I LOVE YOU, DAD, PROBABLY MORE THAN YOU EVER LOVED ME.

ALEXANDRA

MOM,

I KNOW IT HASN'T BEEN EASY LIVING WITH ME THE LAST COUPLE OF YEARS, BUT I HONESTLY TRIED TO TALK TO YOU. I TRIED TO EXPLAIN THE BEST WAY A GIRL MY AGE COULD. YOU STOPPED UNDERSTANDING ME A LONG TIME AGO. I WISH WE COULD HAVE HAD MORE TIME TOGETHER. I HOPE SOME DAY YOU UNDERSTAND THAT NO AMOUNT OF MONEY SHOULD BE ENOUGH TO PAY SOMEBODY TO DO THE WRONG THING. I'VE DONE SOMETHING WRONG, AND I TRIED TO TELL YOU ABOUT IT, BUT YOU WEREN'T THERE. I JUMPED A GIRL WITH TWO OF MY FRIENDS. SHE WAS HURT REALLY BAD. SHE

DIDN'T DIE, BUT I'VE FELT TERRIBLE EVER SINCE IT HAPPENED.

I KNEW WHEN I WAS IN 6TH GRADE THAT I DIDN'T FIT IN WITH THE KIDS IN OUR NEIGHBORHOOD. I TRIED TO EXPLAIN THAT TO YOU AND DAD, BUT YOU NEVER LISTENED TO ME. I'M NOT GOING TO TRY TO FIT IN ANYMORE. FITTING IN ALMOST COST A GIRL HER LIFE. NOW I'M GOING TO FREELY GIVE UP MINE. HAVE A GOOD LIFE, MOM, AND DON'T START SMOKING.

ALEXANDRA

PS. BUY ME A NEW FRILLY DRESS FOR MY GOING HOME DAY. I WANT PEOPLE TO SEE ME HOW I WAS ON THE INSIDE.

Alexandra folded the letters in half and wrote each parent's names on the outside in big black marker. Alexandra walked over to her closet and dug into the back of the closet and pulled out one of her favorite frilly dresses from when she was in 8th grade. She never could wear it outside because the kids picked on her too much. But when she was by herself, Alexandra knew how much she loved the dress. Alexandra went into the bathroom and took a shower. She dried herself off and put on matching underwear. She put on the yellow sundress. It was supposed to come just above the ankle, but now it was closer to Alexandra's knee. Alexandra took one last look at herself in the mirror. Peach fuzz was growing on her head though she had just shaved it a couple of days ago. She went over to her nightstand and put the twenty pills in her hand. She put them all in her mouth and drank them down with a warm cup of juice from the day before. Alexandra lay upon the bed, put both hands clasped on her belly and waited to die.

****

When the other paramedics arrived at the scene, Ashe called Detective Stewart's cell phone.

"I just found Jessica," he blurted.

"Where are you?" Detective Stewart asked.

"I'm in the same vacant lot where we found Tashera. Jessica was dumped here. I guess last night some time."

"How bad is she?"

"She was beat up pretty bad, but I didn't feel any broken bones. She was dehydrated and fairly disoriented."

"How soon before you think she'll be able to talk?"

"After some rest and an IV—four to six hours."

"Great. Thanks for letting me know."

"Stew, I didn't call anybody else within the police to let them know that she'd been found."

"I'll handle that, don't worry," Detective Stewart said.

****

Sheila Odom made pancakes and eggs for Khalil and Tashera, hoping it would remind them of the big Sunday breakfasts that they had when their father was still alive.

At their last breakfast as a family, Kevin Odom ranted and raved about how a new market was opening up with his trucking company, and he'd been offered a supervisor position.

"It's finally the break we need to get out of this housing project," Kevin said.

"It ain't so bad here," Sheila said.

"The kids need to be around a better environment. I want my kids to see people who are successful and know that they can be successful."

Kevin was always a dreamer, Sheila thought. On his way home from work that Sunday, Kevin had a heart attack. He was probably thirty pounds overweight and didn't really exercise—a recipe for disaster. But he was only thirty-five. No one believed a thirty-five-year-old man could have a heart attack until they attended Kevin's funeral.

Sheila never recovered from the loss of her husband. He was the only person who encouraged her to be a better person and that it was okay to want more than what you had. If Kevin was still alive, Sheila wouldn't be facing assault charges, and Khalil wouldn't be a part of a gang.

As they ate their pancakes, Sheila turned on the television. SPECIAL NEWS REPORT flashed across the screen. Sheila turned up the volume and the news reporter said, "Jessica Barnes, the sixteen-year-old girl who was reported missing two days ago was found early this morning in a vacant lot in South East."

The television program showed tape of the lot.

"That's exactly where I was when I got jumped," Tashera said.

"Really?" Sheila asked.

"Yeah. I hope this means they'll let Ahmed go now."

"What are you talking about?" Khalil asked.

"The police arrested him because he threatened Jessica before she went missing. They think he took her, but we all know he didn't," Tashera said and turned her lip up at Khalil.

"Who do you think did it?" Sheila asked.

"Are you serious, Mom?" Tashera asked, getting up from the table.

"Yeah, do you know something I don't?"

Apparently, I do, Tashera thought.

"Let's just be glad she was found," Khalil said, unconvincingly.

"Why should we care about that?" Sheila asked. "She didn't care when she put her hands on Tashera."

"Yeah, you're right. But now that she's found, we can press charges against her and send her up to juvie with the other chick."

"How do you know the other girl is in the detention center?"

"The detective told me."

"Well, it was three of them. It looks like it's two down, one more to go, huh?" Sheila said.

"This is not a bowling game," Tashera said.

"What happened to the third girl, I wonder," Sheila said.

"I know. What happened to her?" Khalil asked.

"Well, if we keep reading the paper or watching the news, maybe we'll find out," Tashera said and walked upstairs in a huff.

Chapter 30

Jessica had been in the hospital about five hours before she woke up. Her body and face were still sore, but she wasn't hungry. She'd been fed nutrients from an IV since she arrived to the emergency room. When she opened her eyes, her mother was the first person that she saw, then she heard someone say, "Jessie, I've been praying for you and praying for you. I knew you'd pull through." Jessica remembered that voice. It was her grandmother, her mother's mother. Whenever she saw Jessica—which hadn't been much since Jessica entered high school, she'd tell Jessica that she was praying for her. Jessica didn't understand why old people always said they were praying for you. Did it make any difference?

Jessica put her hands up to her face and felt the swelling and the cuts. They didn't matter. Jessica was thankful that she was safe.

Detective Stewart walked into Jessica's room while her mother helped her adjust the pillows on her bed.

"Good morning, ladies. I'm Detective Stewart, I'm with the District 7 police station." He flashed his badge. "I would like to ask Jessica a few questions."

"Is that okay, Jessica?" her mother asked.

Jessica nodded her head.

"Did Ahmed Warner kidnap you?"

"No." Jessica frowned and shook her head a little.

"He called you several times on the day that you were kidnapped. Do you know why?"

"He wanted to apologize for our relationship."

"I didn't realize you all were dating," Detective Stewart said.

"We aren't," she said and paused. "He broke up with me in a bad way last summer. He wanted to apologize for that."

"Do you know who did this to you? Did you see the people who beat you up?"

"No." Jessica closed her eyes.

"Are you okay, baby?" her mother asked.

Jessica slowly nodded and opened her eyes.

"We want to find who did this to you," Detective Stewart said and stepped away from the bed.

"Um, Detective?" Jessica said.

"Yeah," Detective Stewart said.

"I want to confess," Jessica said wiping her forehead. "I was one of the girls who attacked Tashera last Monday. It was my idea."

"What are you saying?" Jessica's mother asked.

"After everything I went through, I want to clear my head." Jessica swallowed and took a deep breath. "I don't want to carry it around with me. I shouldn't have attacked her, but I did."

Just then a machine that Jessica was connected to started beeping. A doctor and two nurses rushed in.

"Clear the room," the doctor said. "Her blood pressure is shooting through the roof. We need to stabilize her."

Jessica's eyes rolled to the back of her head and she passed out.

****

Mrs. Warner raced to the station and when Ahmed was released to her, she pulled him into a hug so tight and for so long that Ahmed had to chuckle.

"You're embarrassing me, Mom," he said.

On the way home, Mrs. Warner turned to her son and asked, "You're serious about Tashera, huh?"

"You could say that."

"I want you to say it. I want you tell me what's going on."

"You don't want to know. You don't want to hear it," Ahmed said.

Mrs. Warner pulled the car off to the side of the road. "I want to know what's going on with you."

Ahmed turned to face his mother, anger etched on his face. "Okay," he said, "I hate DC. You moved me here with you because of your job, but I don't want to be here. When I was in Charlotte, you didn't have the people beefin' like you do here. They beef at clubs when they hear songs. They beef for the littlest things. Me and Mike almost came to blows because I didn't call the police on this situation. It's crazy. It's like the city is on some purple pill. I want to move."

"You'll be graduating soon. You'll be going to Temple, so you won't be in DC anyway. Isn't that good enough?"

"I may not come visit you when I leave. I'll probably just go to Charlotte on the holidays and see Dad."

"I can't believe you just said that."

"Mom, look around. Open your eyes. This city has cancer all up and through it. Me and Tashera—we're getting out of here as soon as we can."

As soon as the words left his mouth, Ahmed realized that he hadn't come up with a real plan to get Tashera to leave DC with him. But after seeing his girlfriend's scars from being jumped, witnessing Jessica get snatched, after almost fighting with his best friend over nothing, after going to jail for something he had nothing to do with, Ahmed knew he had to take Tashera and himself out of this environment or he'd risk losing who he was and risk losing her in the process.

"Can I use your cell phone?" Ahmed said. "Mine is dead."

His mother gave him her cell phone. Ahmed dialed Tashera's number.

"Hello?"

"Hey. How are you today?"

"Did they let you out?" Tashera asked, anxiety in her voice.

"Yeah, everything is cool. Can you come over my house?"

"When?" Tashera asked.

"As soon as possible."

"I gotta ask my mom for the car, but I should be able to. I'll call you when I'm on my way."

"Good, it's important."

Ahmed hung up and gave his mother back her cell phone.

"I understand how you feel," Mrs. Warner said, "but I can't just leave the area because you don't like it."

"I know, but I can," Ahmed said and smiled. The basketball department at Temple University told Ahmed to tell them if he needed anything. Now, he did need something. He needed an early escape plan.

****

Ms. Kent parked her car in the garage. It was noon, much later than the time she'd promised her daughter Alexandra that she'd be home.

Alexandra is so needy, she thought. She probably wanted to tell her about some foolishness with her friends

173

again. Ever since Alexandra was little, she'd never really been able to make friends. Ms. Kent thought all the other girls were jealous of Alexandra because she was light skin and pretty.

Ms. Kent opened the door and called Alexandra's name.

"Alex, I'm home." Ms. Kent walked through the family room and the living room. She stopped in the kitchen and looked for Alexandra.

"The girl is probably still sleep," Ms. Kent said and smiled.

Ms. Kent walked in Alex's room and began to whisper, "Alex, it's noon, you know your behind needs to be up."

Alexandra didn't move.

"Alex," Ms. Kent said louder.

She walked over to Alex and shook her shoulders, but Alex didn't respond.

"Alex, Alex, Alex!" she screamed.

Ms. Kent picked up a house phone and called 911.

"My daughter won't wake up," she yelled. "I'm shaking her shoulders. She doesn't respond."

"How old is she?"

"She's 16."

"Have you tried CPR?"

"No?"

Ms. Kent put the phone down, pinched Alexandra's nose, and blew into her mouth. Nothing happened. Ms. Kent picked up the phone again.

"Nothing's happening. Her body is cold. Her body is cold." She sobbed.

"We'll send someone to your address right away."

Ms. Kent sat on the side of the bed and cried as she stared into the lifeless face of her daughter. Even in her grief, she could not help but to notice the slight smile Alexandra wore.

Chapter 31

Tashera pulled up in front of Ahmed's house. Before she could get out of the car, he had jumped down the steps and hugged her.

"Why are you so happy?" Tashera asked.

"It's called being free!" Ahmed smiled and the dimple in his right cheek appeared.

He is so fine, Tashera thought.

Tashera and Ahmed went into the living room where they were surrounded by trophies, ribbons, and medals from Ahmed's illustrious basketball career.

"I told my mom," Ahmed said.

"You told your mom what?"

"I told her that I'm moving."

Tashera saw the wide smile across Ahmed's face. She wanted someone to let her in on his secret joy.

"I thought she knew about your scholarship."

"No, I told her that I want us—me and you—to move away from DC."

"Why'd you tell her that? I don't have a scholarship anywhere."

"Don't you get it, Tashera? I don't have to go to Temple. I can go to a school where they'll make you an offer, too. I want us to do it together."

Tashera stood and looked out the front door.

"I don't know, Ahmed. This is kinda deep."

Ahmed came up to Tashera from behind.

"Everything that has happened this week made me rethink the environment that I want to be around. I was in jail

176

for kidnapping somebody I'd never even laid a finger on. I don't have time for DC. It's a black hole."

"My family is here. What am I supposed to do? Leave them?"

"I am, and I don't care if I don't ever come back. I'm not from DC. I don't owe DC my life. If you don't feel that way, I understand. But as soon as I graduate, I'm outta here. I'm talking to the recruiters tomorrow. If you want to be with me, then you need to make your move; otherwise, I'm going solo."

"It's like that?" Tashera asked.

"Yeah, I don't want anybody but you, but if you can't come with me, I gotta leave you behind. As far as DC is concerned, it's time to go."

"It's time for me to go, too," Tashera said and quickly left Ahmed's house.

Ahmed's incident in jail had truly changed him. Maybe he had gone through too much in six days. Tashera smiled at the thought of Ahmed's willingness to negotiate his scholarship to include an opportunity for her.

No one had ever offered her a way out of the violence that had consumed DC. No one since her father had remotely mentioned that she deserved more than to be preoccupied with the violence that devoured the city. Her mother had become embroiled in revenge against DeCalia's mother, and her brother was more interested in protecting the image of Deuce Trés than caring about what his sister wanted.

Maybe it was time for Tashera to come up with her evacuation plan.

****

At Fitz's house, Khalil put a lighter to the picture of Jessica. The picture turned black as it burned. He looked at the pictures of Alexandra and DeCalia. He knew that

DeCalia was already in Oak Hill Detention Center. He knew he could find a Deuce Trés member that was probably in Oak Hill, but he wasn't sure if he wanted to involve someone else in his revenge. He put the picture of DeCalia back in his pocket. He flipped the picture of Alexandra over and read her address. She lived in the new built-up area in Southeast—the area off of Stanton and Alabama avenues. He stared at her picture.

"It's your turn," he mumbled. "Yo Fitz."

"Yeah," Fitz came back inside. He'd been out back smoking a cigarette.

"Run me over to Alabama and Stanton."

"Cool."

Khalil and Fitz got in the car and drove to the area by Alexandra's house. When they pulled up, there was an ambulance outside, a coroner's car, and a police car.

"It's hot up here," Khalil said.

"Wanna turn around?" Fitz asked.

"Nah, I need you to go pass a specific house. Keep going straight."

Khalil looked at the picture of Alexandra and looked for the address that matched what was written on the back.

"Stop," Khalil said.

Fitz pulled over just as the coroner's staff took a body out of the house that Khalil had been looking for.

Could the girl already be dead? Khalil wondered. He would be sure to read the newspaper tomorrow and find out whose body was taken out of the house.

****

Mr. Ryland was relieved to know that Jessica had been found though she had been beaten. He planned to visit her in the hospital, but he was more sure than ever that someone should check up on Alexandra. After attending church at Union Temple and having brunch with a few friends, Mr. Ryland drove to Marion Barry High and looked up Alexandra's address.

The sun was shining brightly when he'd pulled up in front of Alexandra's house. There were a couple of cars out front of her house.

Mr. Ryland knocked on the door and a thin white man answered.

"Hello, I'm Mr. Ryland, the principal at Alexandra's school. Is her mother here?"

"She's sedated right now."

"Oh. Okay, well, I was really here to check on Alexandra. I've been somewhat worried about her lately with everything that's been going on at school."

"Alexandra passed away last night."

Mr. Ryland felt like someone had elbowed him in the mouth and knocked him square on his tailbone. He grabbed a hold of the rail to keep his balance.

"You can come in," the man said. "I'm Joseph Pedecki. I'm Bonita's co-worker. I rushed over after she called me."

"Could you tell me what happened?" Mr. Ryland said, his voice barely above a whisper.

"All I know is Alexandra committed suicide."

"No. This can't be," Mr. Ryland said. "This can't be. Something was telling me to check on her and I didn't listen."

Mr. Ryland put his hands up to his face. How would he face the rest of his students knowing that he didn't save Alexandra when he sensed she was in danger? How could he ever make up for this?

****

Anita Thomas walked through the broken glass still on her living room floor. If DeCalia was home, she could have told her to clean up the shards. Her thirteen-year-old son Li'l Tommy was too wild and busy running the streets and being down with the Deuce Five crew to be bothered with helping his mother clean up the house.

Anita went into the kitchen and stared at the newspaper that detailed the fight between she and Sheila. She wasn't over it, and she was still determined to make Sheila pay for coming into her house and ruining her furniture. She knew that Sheila didn't have extra money, but she could make her pay in other ways.

Anita had overheard someone mention Laurel Hospital when she was in the courthouse. So Anita assumed that Sheila must have worked there. Anita called information, got the number to hospital, and called.

"Operator."

"I want to file a complaint against one of your workers," Anita said.

"You need to talk to the human resources division, but they're closed on Sundays." The operator gave her the number and said, "They open up at eight a.m."

Anita looked down at the number that she'd written down on her napkin.

This is gonna be easy, she thought.

Chapter 32

Monday, April 9
Seven days after the attack

By seven a.m., Richard King had already told his secretary the essential elements for the judge's letter to drop Sheila's case. Within thirty minutes, the letter would be faxed to the judge's office. Richard was tenacious when it came to his work.

Anita Thomas allegedly throwing a brick through Sheila's window was particularly troubling to him, and it was one of the reasons that Richard resisted taking these kinds of cases from low-income clients.

In the past thirteen years that he'd practiced law, people who had the least amount of resources also had the least amount to lose. Two people fighting in the projects would fight to the death while a rich man would stop fighting another rich man as soon as he felt the fight cost too much. The rich man didn't want to lose his house or his ability to send his kids to private school. But the poor man was already poor. If he were mad enough, he'd fight you until his last breath.

Richard had seen poor folks fight over a bucket of chicken, and the person who won the fight was the person who didn't have the most stab wounds. Richard didn't really believe that having Sheila's lawsuit dropped would stop Anita from harassing her if that's what Anita chose to do. From where Richard was sitting, Anita had nothing to lose.

****

After the first period bell rung, Mr. Ryland came onto the intercom system of Marion Barry High School.

"All juniors and seniors and teachers of 11th and 12th grade students report to the auditorium at once. You have three minutes to get there," Mr. Ryland said in a solemn voice.

Mr. Ryland had not told any teachers or students that there would be an assembly today. The hallways were filled with whispers and rumors of what the assembly was all about.

Mr. Ryland walked on stage and stood before the podium.

"Let me have your attention," Mr. Ryland said. Students continued to file into the auditorium. "Please be seated and be quiet."

Mr. Ryland signaled the a/v tech to shut all the lights off in the auditorium. The students quieted. Behind his head, a giant screen flashed Alexandra's 11th grade school photo.

"This girl who is pictured behind me—this sixteen-year-old young lady who is pictured behind me is dead," Mr. Ryland said.

Gasps were heard in the auditorium.

"Something happened to her. I don't know when and I don't know why, but something made this girl want to take her own life."

The picture behind Mr. Ryland's head changed to a photo of Alexandra when she was in the sixth grade. She was pictured wearing a frilly dress and long hair.

"Where did this girl go? Does anybody know where this girl went?"

Mr. Ryland looked at the picture of Alexandra.

"News reports are going to start appearing on every local station. This school is going to be put under close scrutiny. People are gonna ask what kind of school is Marion Barry High. In one week, we've had a student jumped in broad daylight, a student snatched from her front porch, our star athlete taken to jail, one of our students sent to Oak Hill, and now one of our students has committed suicide..."

Mr. Ryland paused.

"The media is gonna ask what kind of people attend Marion Barry High. Why are they so violent? They are going to ask are they learning anything. They are going to ask what are they doing over in Marion Barry High. What are you going to say? What can we say for ourselves? Did we not all contribute to the things that have gone on in the past week? Well, did we?" Mr. Ryland asked, his voice louder.

"Students, you have some decisions to make. You must decide who you are going to be. If Marion Barry High students continue to find themselves in these predicaments, there will be no Marion Barry High. The government will surely come and plow this school down.

"Alexandra Kent is dead. DeCalia Thomas is in Oak Hill. Which one of you is next? Which one of you wants to be next?"

Junior and senior class pictures were shown on the screen behind Mr. Ryland's head.

"It's coming for you. Are you going to submit to violence? Are you going to give your life away?" Mr. Ryland asked and paused. "You're excused."

****

Ahmed had listened to Mr. Ryland's speech. He couldn't believe the quiet girl who'd asked him had he seen Jessica was dead. He leaned with one leg on the wall as he waited for his next class to start. His ex-best friend Mike came up to him.

"Ahmed, can I talk to you for a minute?" Mike asked.

"Go 'head."

"My fault with everything that went down in the gym on Saturday."

"It's whatever man. I ain't sweatin' that."

"I'm just tryna say, you still my boy and I was just lunchin'. We cool?" Mike asked.

Ahmed nodded.

Mike extended his hand and gave Ahmed a pound.

Ahmed went into his classroom and knew that Mike was being fake. Mike was only trying to be cool with him because Jessica was found, Alexandra was dead, and he didn't have anything over his head. As far as Ahmed was concerned, Mike showed his true colors that day in the gym—colors that Ahmed would never forget.

Ahmed was more concerned with what Tashera was going to do. She hadn't called him at all last night. He sensed that she was mad at him because of his leaving DC talk yesterday. Today, though, he had planned to call at least three of the recruiters that were hot on his trail and tell them about Tashera. Even if they weren't together forever, it made sense to leave DC and start somewhere else with someone whom you cared about and trusted. After Ahmed realized that he couldn't trust Mike, Tashera was the only one left he felt that he could trust. What was Tashera gonna do with that trust?

****

Anita called the Laurel Hospital Human Resources Department around nine-thirty in the morning and stated that she wanted to file a complaint against Sheila Odom.

"I have to transfer you to the supervisor."

When the supervisor came on the line, Anita went into her practiced spiel. "I've been getting several threatening phone calls from Sheila Odom," she began. "First, she came to my house and attacked me. You may have read that in the *Washington Post* a couple of days ago. Well now she's calling and threatening me. She said if I go to the police and say anything that she'd come to my house again. So much of the furniture in my house is broken up already. I don't know what to do." She faked a sob.

"Ms. ... I'm sorry. What's your name?"

"Anita Thomas."

"I'm sorry, Ms. Thomas. I'll do what I can to get to the bottom of this."

Anita hung up and started chuckling.

Getting back at Sheila Thomas is gonna be fun, she thought.

****

Tashera had tossed and turned all night thinking about leaving the area to be with Ahmed. She had never really thought of leaving DC after graduation. She'd figured that she'd work at a salon doing braids or weaves and that'd be it. The thought of leaving DC sort of scared her. She didn't know any place else. Her telephone rang, and she saw Ahmed's name on the Caller ID.

"Hey Ahmed," Tashera said.

"One of the girls who jumped you—Alexandra—she's dead."

"What?"

"She's dead."

Tashera was stunned. She didn't know what to say. One of the girls who attacked her was kidnapped and now another one was dead.

"I gotta go," Tashera said and hung up.

Tashera ran into her mother's room as tears streamed down her face.

"He killed her. He killed her."

Sheila sat up in her bed. "What are you talking about? Calm down."

"One of the girls who jumped me is dead. Ahmed just told me. She's dead."

Tashera was crying hysterically.

"Khalil and his crew did this. I know they did this, Mom. They kidnapped the other girl, too."

"Calm down, Tashera. Calm down."

"No, you calm down. People are dying!"

Tashera went back into her room and slammed the door.

Tashera called Ahmed on the phone.

"Hello."

"I'm ready to move. Tell your recruiters that we're a package deal. Whatever I have to do, I'll do it. I just can't be here anymore."

Tashera went into her closet and looked at her savings account booklet. She had over seven thousand dollars in the bank—monies she'd saved from doing hair over the years. Whether she got into a college or not, she could afford an apartment for a year, an apartment that was a long way from DC.

****

Mr. Ryland sat in his office and typed the beginning of a resignation letter. He planned to submit it to the school board by the end of the week. This experiment with him running Marion Barry High had not turned out well. He didn't seem to have the effect on the students that he wanted to have. The phone in his office rang and he picked it up.

"Mr. Ryland, there's a collect call from DeCalia Thomas. Do you want to speak with her?"

"Yes, put it through," Mr. Ryland said. "How are you, DeCalia?"

"Fine."

Mr. Ryland couldn't bring himself to tell DeCalia about her friend Alexandra's death. Maybe her mother would tell her about it.

"I thought a lot about what you said," DeCalia said. "I'm ready to get out of here."

"Are you ready to change the prosecutor's mind about you?"

"Yeah. What do I have to do?"

"Now that you're willing to fight for yourself, I'll call your attorney and find out."

"Mr. Ryland?"

"Yes."

"You gotta get me out of here."

"As fast as I can," Mr. Ryland said and hung up.

Mr. Ryland imagined the things that must have happened to DeCalia since she first entered Oak Hill. He knew he'd heard fear and desperation in DeCalia's voice. He had to help her and save her in a way that he'd failed with Alexandra.

Chapter 33

Tuesday, April 10
Eight days after the attack

Tashera went into Khalil's room around six in the morning. He wasn't there. More and more, Khalil had begun to spend nights away from the house. Tashera went over to Khalil's dresser and reached in the back of the bottom drawer. Khalil kept knives of all sizes there. Tashera felt the pearl-handle switchblade and pulled it out. Khalil had shown Tashera the switchblade along time ago. By a mere push of the button, the blade popped up lightning fast. If the doctor cleared Tashera to go to school, this was the switchblade she'd carry with her.

****

Anita had her knock-off Louis Vuitton head rag tied tightly around her head when Detective Stewart knocked on her door in the morning. It was late enough for all school age kids to be in school and early enough for the unemployed to answer the phone, "Don't call me this early."

"Hello, Ms. Thomas," Detective Stewart said.

"Hey." Anita leaned on the door and didn't pretend to act like she planned to allow Detective Stewart into her home.

"I need to ask you some questions." Detective Stewart heard loud noises from inside of the house. "Can I come in?"

188

Anita rolled her eyes and pulled the door back.

Detective Stewart walked in and toward the television. A boy sat in front of the television with a game controller in his hand.

"Why is he at home?" Detective Stewart asked.

"He sick."

"He doesn't look sick to me. What's wrong with you, son?" Detective Stewart asked.

"Don't call me son. You ain't my daddy."

"Well, where is your daddy?"

The boy didn't respond.

"Ms. Thomas, what's your son's name?"

"Tommy."

Detective Stewart chuckled to himself and smiled a little. *This woman named her son Thomas Thomas*, he thought. *Unbelievable.*

"Tommy, did you tell your mom you were sick today?"

Tommy kept playing the video game while he asked, "Why you sweatin' me?"

Detective Stewart snatched the game control out of Tommy's hand.

"If you're sick, you shouldn't be playin' games."

"I ain't sick, but my shoulder hurts. That's all."

Detective Stewart looked at Tommy's left shoulder and then walked around him and looked on his right. Tommy had on a wide bandage that had blood and pus seeping from it.

Detective scrunched his face, dug into his pockets, and put on his rubber gloves.

"Tommy, sit on the couch over there by the light," he said. "I need to look at your shoulder."

Tommy looked back at his mom. She just looked away.

Detective Stewart lifted up the bandage and saw what looked like a homemade tattoo that was completely infected with blood and pus oozing from every pore.

"Who did you let do this tattoo? Your whole arm is infected. You need to go to the hospital and get some antibiotics, now."

Detective Stewart looked at Anita. "You're his mother. You need to take him to the hospital."

"I didn't tell him to get that tattoo in the first place," Anita said. "His arm needs to fall off if he stupid enough to let anybody write on his body, anyway."

"Tommy, what's this tattoo supposed to say?" Detective Stewart asked.

"Deuce Five," Tommy said.

Detective Stewart shook his head. Tommy Thomas was thirteen years old, but he could have easily passed for eleven, and he was already a tattooed member of Deuce Five. Gang recruitment was getting younger and younger, and it seemed that the gang prevention departments at the police station were completely ineffective.

"I'll give you and your mom a ride to the hospital, so go upstairs and put on a real shirt over that tank top."

Tommy and Anita went upstairs and Detective Stewart waited for them to return. Anita came back downstairs first, still with the rag on her head, but in jeans and a sweatshirt.

"Did you know he's already a part of Deuce Five?" Detective Stewart asked.

"No."

Detective Stewart wanted to tell Anita that she was not going to win parent of the year anytime soon and that she needed to stop being a slacker, but instead he focused on the real reason that he'd come to her house.

"Did you throw a brick threw Sheila Odom's window last Friday?"

"No," Anita said without giving Detective Stewart eye contact.

"I think you're lying."

"You got some witnesses or something?"

"No."

"Well then it don't matter what you think."

"Look Ms. Thomas. I'm here because this situation with you and Sheila Odom needs to go away. It's minor. She came here because your daughter—who confessed—attacked hers. Maybe she got hot. Maybe she got testy, but she came here because she was in a bad way about her daughter. Can't you understand that?"

"She put her hands on me when she came here. That was uncalled for."

"But what DeCalia did was uncalled for. Somebody has to back down."

"It ain't gonna be me," Anita said.

"You want to go to jail over this?"

"I ain't afraid of jail."

"I didn't say you were afraid. I asked you if you want to go to jail."

"It's whatever, man. Whatever happens. Whatever."

Tommy bounced down the steps and Detective Stewart and Anita got up.

"Let's go to the hospital," Detective Stewart said, frustrated. He had met so many people who didn't care about the things that happened to them in their lives. Many of them seemed to be drug addicts, uneducated, sufferers of an impoverished mentality, or just plain lazy. From what he could see of Anita, she was at least three out of four.

The department was not going to waste money putting a detail on Anita to see if she'd tried to throw another brick. The only way the department would get involved in another incident with Anita and Sheila was after it happened.

In what police departments deemed minor cases, there was no such thing as prevention.

****

Khalil avoided going home yesterday when his mother told him that Tashera thought he killed Alexandra. His mother explained that Tashera was "emotional" and that she "wasn't thinking clearly." Though Tashera had told his mother about him being involved with Jessica's kidnapping as well, his mother didn't bother to ask him if he was involved. Khalil realized when he was about thirteen years old that his mother would always take his side, even when he was wrong. It was a destructive kind of security blanket. Instead of his mother's confidence in him making him want to stand-up and be a real man, he hid behind her naïveté and allowed her to make excuses for him—even when his sister was right about him.

Yesterday, he made some calls to other members of Deuce Trés. He wanted to find out how many members they had in Oak Hill. He figured if they had any girls in the facility, he'd talk them into attacking DeCalia, and if they only had boys in the facility, he figured they could sweet talk a couple of girls to jump her.

He'd recalled that Jessica said that the only person who kicked his sister was DeCalia, and he was gonna make sure he returned the favor.

****

Tashera and her mom went to the doctor's office that morning.

"You still have significant swelling near your reproductive organs, but it doesn't look like there'll be permanent damage," the doctor said.

"Thank God," Sheila said out loud.

"Now I can have bunches of kids," Tashera said then added "Sike! I don't want no babies."

Tashera let out a little chuckle. After the doctor looked at Tashera's ribs, she was cleared to return to Marion Barry High. She was glad. She was tired of being at home with Khalil and his treacherous ways, and she was tired of watching her mom pretend to not notice or worse—pretend not to care. In the drive over to Marion Barry High, Tashera thought about what Ahmed had said.

"Mom," she said, "when I graduate in two months, I'm moving out."

"Where are you going?"

"I'm going to a summer school pre-college program and then to college in the fall."

"I thought you were going to go to UDC or Prince George's Community College to get started," Sheila said.

"Nah. I don't think so."

"Do you know where you're going?"

"Pennsylvania, North Carolina, or Georgia. I should know in a month or so. I'll keep you posted."

"How are you gonna pay for your tuition and living expenses?"

"I saved some money and I'll probably be able to get a scholarship or something. Whatever's leftover, I can get a student loan or something. I just gotta get away."

"You're all ready to leave us behind, huh?"

Tashera didn't respond. The more she had thought about leaving DC, the more she really believed that it was a good idea. Her mother and brother seemed stuck. Even after Tashera's father died, her mother had made enough money to move the family into a new neighborhood. When her mother finally got up the resources to move, Khalil got shot. The money that was needed to take care of a paraplegic who was going through therapy, in the initial stages, decimated Sheila's savings. Sheila never blamed Khalil for preventing their move into a better environment, but it's exactly what had happened. And Tashera knew it, too.

Sheila pulled in front of Marion Barry High and Tashera exited the car without a word.

****

Ahmed had reached out to three recruiters in his quest to secure a scholarship for him and Tashera: Temple University, University of North Carolina at Wilmington, and Georgia Tech. The recruiter at Temple University gave him a hard time from the gate.

"It's gonna be tight trying to get you and somebody else in here on essentially the same scholarship," the recruiter said.

"It's not the same scholarship. I thought you had something like the buddy system."

"That's more for two student athletes."

"Either you're gonna make this happen or you're not," Ahmed said.

"Have your friend go online and download all of the application forms. Once she gets those done, have her call me," the recruiter said and hung up.

Ahmed left messages with the recruiters at the other schools. He still awaited their return calls.

Ahmed stood, emptying some books in his locker when he felt a warm hand touch the small of his back. He pulled away quickly. He knew a touch like that could be misconstrued if Tashera saw it. He turned around and couldn't believe that Tashera was standing there. He hugged her and lifted her off the ground at the same time.

"What are you doing here?" Ahmed asked.

"I go here, remember?"

"You didn't tell me that you were coming back today."

"I wanted to surprise you. I wanted to see if I was gonna catch you out there."

"Yeah, and what did you see?" Ahmed paused. "You saw a brother mindin' his own business. I want to walk you to class. Where are you headed now?"

"I haven't even signed in yet. I gotta go to the office first."

"Let's go," Ahmed said.

"Have you found out anything about the schools yet?"

"They want you to apply and it looks like they'll review your grades and it'll be on from there."

"You sound awfully confident."

"I know my girl ain't no dummy. This will be a breeze for you."

Ahmed and Tashera stopped in front of the office, and Ahmed leaned down and kissed Tashera on the lips.

****

Mr. Ryland sat in his office, perplexed about what to do to get DeCalia out of Oak Hill.

He didn't want to call the lawyer or the Community Prosecutor until he had a plan that he thought they wouldn't be able to say no to. As an NBA player, Mr. Ryland saw all kinds of negotiations go down. He saw how popular players received different treatment than players who the league didn't smile upon. He learned that if other players spoke up on your behalf, it seemed to sway the commissioner, the owners, the fans—just about everybody.

195

Mr. Ryland wanted someone to speak up for DeCalia—somebody that the prosecutor would be inclined to listen to. He stood up and walked to the front of his office just as Tashera Odom walked to the front desk.

"Hello Miss Cannon. You're looking fly as usual," Tashera said.

Miss Cannon came from around the desk and hugged Tashera.

"It is so good to see you. You know I prayed for you everyday."

"I know, Miss Cannon. I felt that somebody prayed for me. I should have known it was you."

"Are you back already or just picking up work to take home?"

"I'm back."

Tashera felt a sharp pain shoot through her abdomen. She groaned. "I gotta sit down for a minute," she said.

Miss Cannon sat down next to Tashera.

"Are you okay?" she asked.

"Yeah. I went to the doctor today and he said I'd have shooting pains every now and then until I am completely healed. I gotta get used to it, I guess."

"Well, I'll sign you in, give you a pass, and you can go to your class."

Miss Cannon went back to her desk and started filling out papers. Mr. Ryland stepped outside of his office.

"Tashera?" he said.

"Hi. Mr. Ryland."

"I couldn't help but notice you. Welcome back. Is there anything that I can do to help you get back into the swing of things?"

Tashera looked up at the ceiling. "I could use an escort to class for the next couple of days in case these pains start while I'm walking."

"Got anybody in mind?"

"Sure do. Ahmed Warner."

"Miss Cannon, make sure Ahmed Warner has a pass this week to help Tashera."

"Will do."

That was too easy, Tashera thought. *I guess getting hurt does have some fringe benefits.* Tashera couldn't wait to be holding Ahmed's hand everyday while he walked her from one class to the other.

"I would like to talk to you a minute in my office Tashera," Mr. Ryland said.

"Okay," Tashera said and pushed herself up by the seat of the chair.

Mr. Ryland walked into his office and Tashera followed.

"Do you remember when I came to visit you in the hospital?" he asked as soon as they were seated.

"No. You were there?"

"I stopped in and you were knocked out. I wanted to show support to you and your family."

"Thanks. What do you want to talk to me about?"

"Specifically DeCalia Thomas and Jessica Barnes. Did you know those girls prior to the incident?"

"No."

"You'd never talked to them before?"

"Didn't I just tell you I didn't know them?"

"DeCalia and Jessica are both looking at some hard time in the juvenile facility, and I believe both of them are on the road where they've learned or are beginning to learn their lesson."

"So what do you want from me?"

"When their case is brought before the judge, I would like you to testify on their behalf."

"You want me to do what?" Tashera yelled.

"You know people make mistakes. Alexandra is dead. Jessica was kidnapped and beaten. I don't think she'll be back to school in the next three to four weeks. It seems like a lot of people's lives are being ruined for a mistake that should have never happened."

Tashera's eyes had gone beet red. She couldn't believe this Magic Johnson wanna-be just asked her to help the people who attacked her.

He must be sniffin' the fumes that come out of the Bentley he drives to school everyday, Tashera thought.

"I'm the victim here," she said, "and I can't believe you sat and asked me to help the people who put me in the hospital for no reason. I may not have the physical scars, but don't think for one minute that I don't recall what it felt like to be punched, kicked, and beaten in the middle of a vacant lot."

"I understand what you're saying."

"Obviously, you don't understand how I feel. I just had to sit down because of pains that I felt from this same beating, and you're asking me to help them. I honestly can't think of one reason why I would. As far as I'm concerned, both of them can get thrown under the jail or die."

Tashera's eyes bore into Mr. Ryland like lasers ready to burn through his flesh.

"I'm sorry you feel that way," Mr. Ryland said.

"Nah. You're just sorry."

Tashera stood and left Mr. Ryland's office.

Outside the office, Tashera leaned against the wall and sighed. Mr. Ryland's request swirled around her mind, and she shook her head as if trying to get the request out.

"It was *not* time to come back here," she muttered before walking down the hall.

****

Sheila sat down at her desk in the offices of Laurel Hospital. She couldn't believe it had only been a week since she'd been at work. It seemed more like a month. Before she could turn on her computer and check her messages good, Nancy Bilbow, Mr. Kotowsky's secretary stopped by her desk.

"You need to report to Mr. Kotowsky's office right away," she said.

"Me?" Sheila asked. "Are you sure?"

"Yes, I'm sure," Nancy said.

Sheila grabbed her purse and got on the elevator to Mr. Kotowsky's office.

A different receptionist had her wait fifteen minutes before she was escorted into Kotowsky's plush-carpeted, wall paneled office.

"Hello Sheila," Mr. Kotowsky said.

"How are you?"

Kotowsky sat behind his desk. He stared at Sheila for a moment. "What's been going on with you lately?"

"I called in and told my supervisor—my daughter has been in the hospital. She was attacked last week."

"Um, hmm." He lifted his hands up and together, making a church steeple with his fingers.

"What's that supposed to mean?"

"The hospital is concerned about the article in the newspaper about you attacking another woman in her home."

"Why is the hospital worried about that?"

"It looks bad for us. You're one of our employees."

"What I do on my own time is my business."

Mr. Kotowsky released a light chuckle.

"You're wrong on that one," he said. "You need to read your personnel forms again. If an employee acts in a way that can bring bad light onto the hospital, we are within our right to suspend and even dismiss that employee."

"What are you saying?"

"You're being suspended for the next three weeks, pending further investigation. Drop your badge off with my secretary on your way out."

Sheila opened her mouth to say something, but she realized that Kotowsky had already dismissed her in his mind. He lifted a pen and began reading the papers before him.

"Ain't this a ..." Sheila mumbled under her breath.

She stomped back to the elevator and collected her personal items from her desk. She even removed the picture of Khalil and Tashera from her desk. The last time that Sheila recalled someone being suspended from Laurel Hospital, they never came back.

On the metro, Sheila thought about the personnel forms that she must have signed. She didn't realize that the altercation with Anita could have impacted her job. With Tashera leaving in a few months, if Sheila lost her job, she and Khalil would be in the worst shape ever.

Chapter 34

Wednesday, April 11
Nine days after the attack

At the recommendation of the judge, Richard and Sheila were scheduled to meet with the Community Prosecutor.

In a conference room down from his office, Sheila rested her hands on the table and sighed.

"My job suspended me yesterday," she said.

"For what?"

"Something about behavior that mars the reputation of the hospital—something that I signed when I was hired. They read the article in the newspaper and felt my actions were worth suspending me."

"Did they say for how long?"

"Right now, it's three weeks. But nobody I know who was ever suspended from there ever came back."

Richard put his hand up to his face.

"Sheila, I don't want to be harsh, but I don't have an unlimited amount of time to work on these cases of yours. I'm doing this one 'cause you're family, but I have a whole schedule of paying clients that I gotta deal with."

Sheila looked at Richard as if he threatened to slap her. "So it's like that?"

"I'll try to draft a letter on your behalf to the hospital, and if this case gets thrown out, that'll help also. I'll put all of that in the letter."

"You're acting like this is my fault. I didn't have anything to do with Tashera getting jumped."

Richard looked at Sheila and exhaled.

"Don't you understand that everything that's happened to you since Tashera got jumped is your fault?" Richard asked calmly.

"The school wasn't doing anything. The police wasn't doing anything."

"Weren't they? Or they weren't doing anything fast enough for you? Which one is it?"

"It's the same thing," Sheila said.

"No, it isn't. The police started investigating immediately. It seems to me that they didn't share every detail with you, but they were looking into the situation. I believe the police have one of the attackers in custody now with another scheduled to be arrested the minute she gets out of the hospital. What do you want them to do, shoot Tashera's attackers in broad daylight?"

"Maybe."

"You wouldn't even be here if you didn't go to the mother's house. You wouldn't have been suspended from your job if you hadn't gone to the mother's house. You need to take a long look in the mirror. A lot of this you brought on yourself."

The Community Prosecutor entered the conference room before Sheila had the opportunity to respond to Richard.

"Good Morning, everyone," Mr. Wellesley said. "Mr. King, what points do you want to make?"

"I don't want us to waste the court's time or tax payer's money," Richard began. "Ms. Odom has no priors. She simply went to Anita Thomas' house to talk. The conversation didn't go well and tempers flared. If this was high school, they'd both be sent to detention, and that would be the end of it.

"We have reason to believe that Anita Thomas threw a brick through Ms. Odom's window a couple of days ago. That matter is being investigated by police. I suggest we do joint restraining orders—of at least 100 feet—and close the case."

"My office is on me to go hard on these kinds of cases because they are such a tremendous waste of time," Wellesley responded.

"There's another case that's been sort of put on hold." Richard tapped his pen against the table before continuing. "It'd be worth a couple of lines in the newspaper. The other girl who attacked Tashera Odom—Ms. Odom's daughter—the real reason we're here—she recently confessed to Detective Stewart. That's what I heard. She's in the hospital right now. It seems to me since DeCalia Thomas is in Oak Hill, they all but forgot about this other girl."

"Why'd they forget about her?" The prosecutor asked.

"Because she was the girl who was missing, but they found her a couple of days ago."

The prosecutor smiled. "The girl could have staged her own disappearance to get away from being charged with assault," he said.

Richard offered the slightest of smiles in return and added, "Could have."

"That would be the top news story this evening if we locked her up." The prosecutor's eyes darted around the room like his brain was calculating things faster than his head could register them all.

"Do you have anything to add, Ms. Odom?" Wellesley asked.

Sheila looked at the prosecutor. She knew it was times like these that determined if the system would look kindly at your case or throw you under the prison. Sheila wanted to tell the prosecutor that he reminded her of the penguin from one of the Batman movies. But instead she said, "No, I have nothing further to add."

"Okay then. I'll let you know by COB today regarding your case and watch the news for the development in your daughter's case. Which detective is investigating the brick incident?"

"Detective Stewart."

"I know who he is. I'll give him a call to verify," Mr. Wellesley said and everyone got up from the table and left the conference room.

The elevator was completely silent when Richard and Sheila rode down to the first floor. The entire ride Sheila thought, *What if Richard is right and this is my fault?* Then she thought, *Nah, this can't be my fault. Somebody had to stand up for Tashera.*

Her grade school teachers had told her hundreds of times that there was a wrong way to fight and a right way. Sheila had begun to question if she'd done the right thing in going to Anita Thomas' house. Visiting her house wasn't worth losing her job over. But now her job was hanging in the balance, and there was nothing she could do about it.

****

Tashera spent all morning submitting the college application forms as Ahmed had suggested. She hoped her grades would allow her to get into college, but she realized that she was applying later than most seniors.

Ahmed met Tashera in the library during their third period study hall.

"I've submitted all the applications and emailed them to your contacts," Tashera said.

"That's good," he said as he took the seat beside her. "They said they'd get back to us as soon as possible. Since we're applying in a buddy system, we won't have to wait long before we know something. Hopefully, we'll know something by the end of the week."

Tashera faced Ahmed. "Mr. Ryland wants me to help the girls who attacked me."

"What?" Ahmed's eyes glinted with anger.

"He was talking some smack about people making mistakes and people's lives getting ruined. I couldn't believe it. He didn't say anything about my life."

"I guess to him you look healed 'cause you're so fine. That's what it is."

Tashera smiled and Ahmed touched her on the chin.

I look healed on the outside, Tashera thought, *but you never get over somebody violating you like that.*

Ahmed dropped a light kiss on Tashera's cheek before standing. "I have to get to class," he said. "I'll check in on your later."

As Ahmed turned and walked away, the smile on Tashera's face fell. Around Ahmed, Tashera always smiled, but inside she felt hatred and anger. She hated the girls who jumped her and the people who probably knew what they were planning and didn't do anything about it. A couple of girls called Tashera and asked if she'd do their hair, but she told them no. She didn't know if they really wanted hair appointments or if they were there to spy on her. In such a short amount of time, Tashera had changed. She'd never be the same, and she knew it even if Ahmed or Mr. Ryland didn't.

Tashera dug around in her backpack for a pen and felt the switchblade that she started bringing to school yesterday. She didn't trust that another group of girls wouldn't try to jump her, and she wasn't about to wait until something happened. This time, she'd be prepared and someone else would be lying on the ground passed out.

She pulled a pen and her notebook from her backpack and begin flipping through it. She had pages of letters that she'd written to Yasmin Shiraz over the last week, and with the anger inside her, an anger that threatened to consume her, Tashera decided to write another and actually send it to Yasmin.

Miss Yasmin,

You visited my school last month in Southeast, DC. I was the girl sitting way in the back with long braids. You probably don't remember me. I didn't say one word during your whole speech. But since you gave us your MySpace address, I checked you out and decided to connect. All that stuff you were saying about choosing the life you want and being positive, it sounds good, but it doesn't work around here. In my 'hood we have people fighting that live two blocks from each other. I live in the Deuce Trés (23rd Street) and we're at war with Deuce Five (25th Street.) If somebody from Deuce Five sees someone from Deuce Trés, a fight can jump off right on the spot. Hearing guns pop off is an every day, every hour situation. I used to have friends in like 3rd grade that lived in the Deuce Five area, but now if I see one of them, they act like they don't know me, and I gotta act

all rumble tumble or they'll try to punk me.
And that's just when I get home. At school,
girls are fighting each other over boys,
what you look like and what you wearing.
I've always tried to be cool with everybody.
Ugly girls, pretty girls, best dressed and
bummy, they've all been my friends--until
nine days ago, when I was coming out the
mini-mart and this girl and two of her
friends jumped me. I don't know why they
jumped me, not really. I would tell you, but
it'd make this letter too long. My point is
you said we could choose the life we
wanted, and I didn't choose to be jumped.
I didn't choose to live in a neighborhood
where people are dying everyday. But that's
exactly where I am. If you say we can
choose our life, you gotta help me choose
something different. 'Cause right now, I'm
carrying a switchblade everywhere I go.
And if the wrong person steps to me, I'm
choosing death- for my enemy.

Your girl,

Tashera

Tashera stood and walked to the office.
"Ms. Cannon, I need to type up this letter," she said.
"May I use your extra computer?"

"Who's the letter to?"

"Yasmin Shiraz. She was here last month doing a self-esteem workshop. I just wrote her e-mail address down from the internet. She said we could write her anytime."

"Sure, go ahead."

Tashera sat, opened her e-mail account in the internet browser, and quickly began to type in the letter.

When she hit SEND and received confirmation of the e-mail's transmission, Tashera placed her palm on the computer screen.

Maybe Ms. Shiraz is some kind of genie or has a crystal ball or something, Tashera thought. *Maybe she can help me to stop feeling this way.*

****

Mr. Ryland went to the hospital to visit Jessica at lunchtime. When he entered her room, she had a bandage wrapped around her head, she was in hospital-issued pajamas, and she had a wrist splint on her arm.

"Hello," Mr. Ryland said as he walked in.

"Hi, Mr. Ryland," Jessica said.

"You know who I am. That's a relief."

"Everybody knows who you are."

"I need to talk to you about what happened with you, DeCalia, and Alexandra."

"I already confessed," Jessica said.

"You spoke with Detective Stewart already?"

"Yeah."

Detective Stewart and Rodriguez walked into Jessica's room with two uniform policemen behind them.

Detective Stewart approached the bed on the left side while Detective Rodriguez stood on the right.

"Jessica Barnes, you are under arrest for suspicion of aggravated assault against Tashera Odom," Stewart stated.

Detective Rodriguez threw some sweatpants and a t-shirt on the bed. "Put these on," she said.

"What's happening?" Jessica cried as the tears started to roll down her face.

"You're not waiting for her injuries to heal before arresting her?" Mr. Ryland asked.

"I know it's unusual," Detective Stewart said, "but it's pressure from the top. Everybody is looking at this case. We gotta take her in."

Jessica hobbled over to the bathroom and changed into the outfit that Detective Rodriguez had given her.

"Mr. Ryland," Jessica said, "please call my mom."

One of the nurses came in Jessica's room with a wheelchair and motioned for Jessica to sit in it. The detectives and two policemen wheeled Jessica to the front of the hospital. When they arrived at the entrance, reporters' questions and photographers' camera flashes attacked the officers and Jessica, and they swiftly made their way to the police car and pulled off.

Mr. Ryland stood by and watched the media frenzy.

"This was a publicity stunt," he said aloud, but no one heard him over the police siren and the flashes and the clicking of the cameras.

****

Khalil and Fitz shot pool at Fast Eddies in Suitland, Maryland. One of Khalil's contacts was scheduled to meet him at the pool hall to let him know how many soldiers they had at Oak Hill. Khalil beat Fitz mercilessly in pool. It was one of the advantages of being in a wheelchair—Khalil was the height of the table, so he saw all the best angles.

Hurt, an overly muscular member of Deuce Trés who belonged in the Mr. World Bodybuilding competition, walked in Fast Eddies and headed directly toward Khalil.

"Hold on," Khalil said to Fitz and rolled into a dark corner with Hurt following him.

"We got a young girl named Renee who just got up there a couple of days ago," Hurt said, "but she ain't a banger."

"What she up there for then?"

"We had her on the block."

"Turnin' tricks? Come on, man. She ain't gonna be able to put this girl down."

Khalil rolled away and picked up his pool stick. He disliked the fact that he wouldn't be able to exact revenge on DeCalia right now.

Khalil remembered how he and Darren used to fight about having young girls in their crew turning tricks.

"What's your problem?" Darren had said. "It's just a piece of meat. She's gonna give it away anyway. Why can't we make some money off of her?"

"You can't bring a female into the crew, kick it to her like she's one of us, then put her out on the track," Khalil had replied. "She won't be loyal to us."

"Then I'll smoke her," Darren said.

They'd come across plenty of girls who were runaways and just wanted to be a part of something. They'd find some of them with their suitcases at Union Station. Darren didn't believe in passing by a pretty face.

Pretty faces ended up being Darren's downfall, Khalil thought. *What will mine be?*

Chapter 35

Thursday, April 12
Ten days after the attack

When Tashera opened her front door to go to school, news reporters, camera crews, and photographers started shouting at her and taking her picture. Apparently they had seen last night's evening newscast, which featured DeCalia's and Jessica's mugshots with the following headline:

THREE DC TEENS ORCHESTRATE BRUTAL ATTACK ON FELLOW STUDENT, ONE COMMITS SUICIDE.

Someone at the courthouse must have tipped them off with her address and so here they were stalking her on the way to school. Tashera walked two blocks to the bus stop with reporters alongside her for every step.

"Are you glad Alexandra Kent is dead?" a reporter asked.

"Did you pay somebody to kidnap Jessica Barnes?" another reporter asked.

"Is it true that you won't be able to bear any children?" came another question.

Sheila saw the line of reporters that had begun to follow Tashera. Sheila ran out the house, jumped into her car, and almost mowed a couple of them over.

"Get in the car," Sheila yelled to Tashera and drove her to Marion Barry High School.

When they pulled up in front of the school, there were a bunch of reporters that had surrounded Ahmed and were seemingly blocking the front entrance.

"They're worst than vultures," Tashera said.

"And hungrier," Sheila added. "Call Ahmed's cell phone and tell him to run over to the car. I'll drive you both to the back entrance."

Tashera did what she was told and within seconds, Ahmed jumped in the back seat of their Camry.

"Thanks Ms. Odom," Ahmed said as he slid into the backseat. "I guess it's going to be a circus until the trial is over."

"That could be forever," Tashera said.

"No. You haven't heard?" Ahmed asked.

"Heard what?" Tashera asked.

"The trial starts today."

"I forgot to tell you, Shera." Sheila said. "The detective called me last night. I'll have to pick you up early from school today, probably."

"I thought you'd be at work."

"They're letting me off so I can deal with this stuff," Sheila said.

Tashera had never heard of a trial starting ten days after an incident, but once the media hailstorm hit, it seemed that the lawmakers wanted Jessica's and DeCalia's heads on two platters. Even the DC mayor was on the news talking about the case.

****

Jessica rested in a private cell that was about the size of her small hospital room. Her mother and her attorney, Harold Stern visited her.

"You have the option to be tried with your friend DeCalia Thomas or for your cases to be severed," Stern said.

"We did it together," Jessica said. "Why would we separate our cases?"

"In this case because you don't have any negative background or criminal record and she has a history of incidents in juvenile court, we could argue that you were under the influence of DeCalia—she has much more experience than you, obviously. Also, you're sixteen and with no priors, we could get your case remanded to juvenile court. She's seventeen and with so many bad school incidents on her record, the prosecutor has a stronger case to try her as an adult."

"The bottom line is you gotta look out for yourself," her mother said.

"But this was my idea—the attack—was my idea," Jessica said.

The attorney looked around. "Don't say that too loud. It doesn't matter whose idea it was. On paper, no one would believe that it was your idea."

Jessica frowned. She and DeCalia were the best of friends. When Jessica started feeling bad about herself after Ahmed passed her around the basketball team, it was DeCalia who was there to tell her to forget about Ahmed. All of Jessica's life she was always expected to be a quiet girl and follow the rules, but when she hooked up with DeCalia, her friend encouraged her to be independent and to go against the rules. It was a freeing feeling for Jessica.

"I don't want us to be separated," Jessica said.

"That's not smart," Mr. Stern said.

"Why would you want to be on the same side as that girl?" her mother asked. "Don't you understand that she'll probably go to jail and be tried as an adult? You can't possibly want to throw your life down the drain, too."

"Mom, I got her into this mess. She had my back. I have to have hers," Jessica said. "Maybe me not having a bad record will help her."

"Jessica, you can't possibly comprehend this situation and what can happen to you."

"I couldn't live with myself if I left DeCalia hanging, Mom."

Lenise Barnes stood and dropped a quick kiss on Jessica's cheek.

"This is your life," she whispered. She stared into Jessica's eyes and added, "I'll go along with your wishes-- for now."

She quickly turned and left the holding cell.

Mr. Stern pulled his chair close to Jessica. "Think about what we're saying," he said. "If the situation were reversed, would DeCalia Thomas throw her life away for you?"

"She already has," she answered.

Jessica understood where her mother and the lawyer was coming from, but she didn't want to hate herself—not like she had when her relationship with Ahmed went bad— not ever again. Maybe she'd get punished for sticking with DeCalia, but she'd be able to look herself in the mirror. That should account for something.

****

Mr. Ryland sat in the conference room with the attorney that he'd hired for DeCalia's defense.

"How's her case look, Dempsey?"

Dempsey flipped through pages in a folder. "She's seventeen," he said. "She's had a bunch of suspensions from school, probation warnings. It's gonna be tough for her to come through without jail time—adult jail time. Why are you so interested in this girl anyway?"

"I came to Marion Barry High believing I could make a difference. Heck, I haven't even been able to make a dent."

"You may not want to hitch your caboose to this train."

Mr. Ryland thought, *The exact thing had been said about me.* Sean Ryland was a knuckleheaded troublemaker before basketball found him. The noise that came from the door opening startled Mr. Ryland from his daydream. Two policemen had escorted DeCalia Thomas into the conference room. When Mr. Ryland walked up to her, he could see new cuts and bruises on her face.

"Who did that to your face?" Mr. Ryland asked.

"I got into a fight."

"You look like you got into a war."

"Have a seat, Ms. Thomas," attorney Dempsey said. As soon as DeCalia's bottom touched a chair, Dempsey began, "They're rushing this case to trial. The mayor, the politicians—they want to send out a message that DC is not soft on crime. I need to prepare you for what's likely to happen."

DeCalia looked at Mr. Ryland. He reached out and grabbed her hand.

"Because you're seventeen, they're going to treat this like an adult case. The worse case scenario is they could send you back to Oak Hill because they house offenders there to the age of twenty-one."

"I don't want to go back there," DeCalia said. Her eyes widened as she reached for Mr. Ryland. "Mr. Ryland, you gotta do something. I don't want to go back there."

"What about probation? Couldn't she get probation and be sent home?" Mr. Ryland asked. "Or even house arrest? Do you think those are options to petition to the court?"

"We can put all of those options on the table, but when the system smells blood, they generally go for the most punitive sentencing possible. With all of the media play, I can't imagine that the judge would truly consider probation or house arrest when the assault charge carries a sentence of ten to twenty years."

Mr. Ryland put his hand on his belt and thought deeply about DeCalia's situation. When DeCalia and her friends decided to jump Tashera Odom, they probably didn't think the tables would turn and the system would want to make an example out of them. The thing with making bad choices was you never knew how the other side was going to react.

****

A policeman escorted attorney Harold Stern and another pushed Jessica's wheelchair into the conference room where DeCalia sat handcuffed at the wrists and ankles. When Jessica saw DeCalia—with all the purplish bruises on her face—all she could say was, "I'm sorry." The officer pushed Jessica to the table, and her attorney sat next to her while all the officers cleared the room.

"I need to speak to DeCalia in private," Jessica said.

"You're under custody," Attorney Dempsey said. "By law we can't leave the room."

"Well, can you back up some?"

The attorneys walked away from the table and gave the girls some space.

"I confessed to everything, so you don't even have to say anything," Jessica said.

"I confessed, too. I said you were there, but that I was the only one hitting and punching her."

"Who'd you confess to?" Jessica asked.

"The detective," DeCalia said.

"Me too."

"Did you have an attorney present?" Jessica's attorney asked.

"I thought this was a private conversation," DeCalia said.

"No, my attorney wasn't there," Jessica said.

216

"Well, the confession gets thrown out."

"Ladies, I know you're trying to figure out what you should do," Stern said. "But we went to law school to create strategies for you. Why don't you let us do our jobs?"

"You're both going to enter a plea of not guilty," Dempsey said. "Don't worry about your confessions. The jury will never hear them."

"Not guilty?" Mr. Ryland asked. "Wait a minute here. Let's not forget that a girl was seriously hurt in this process."

Stern stood and walked over to Mr. Ryland.

"Sean, we appreciate everything that you're doing for the kids at Marion Barry High," he said, "but it's time the lawyers do what's necessary. You're thinking like a principal, and that's fine, but that's not what we're hired to do."

"I know what you're hired to do. I'm paying the retainer for one of y'all," Mr. Ryland said.

"Sean, it might get uncomfortable for you in here while we're setting up strategies," Dempsey added. "Rest assured we're looking out for the best interests of our clients."

Mr. Ryland looked at DeCalia and Jessica, but he thought about Tashera and Alexandra, as well. He didn't want any of his students to become hardened criminals, but he didn't want any of his students to feel that violations against them would go unpunished.

"I'll see you all in court," Mr. Ryland said and walked out of the conference room.

Chapter 36

In the District of Columbia Superior Court Building, DeCalia Thomas and Jessica Barnes sat side by side at the defense table with their lawyers on their opposite sides. Behind them sat Anita Thomas and her son, Li'l Tommy, Lenise Barnes, and a horde of spectators. On the other side of the courtroom, the prosecutor sat flanked by two others at his table. Sheila Odom, Tashera, Khalil, and Detectives Stewart and Rodriguez sat closest to the prosecutor with Mr. Ryland sitting way in the back of the courtroom.

The judge entered the courtroom, a walnut-colored woman with a short, divalicious hairdo. An officer of the court read off the corresponding case numbers, and everyone at the defense table stood.

"How does Jessica Barnes plead to the charge of assault against Tashera Odom?" the judge asked.

"Not guilty," Jessica said from her wheelchair.

"How does DeCalia Thomas plead to the charge of assault against Tashera Odom?"

"Not guilty," DeCalia said.

The judge reviewed some papers on her desk.

"With respect to the court's time, we're going to move this case as swiftly as possible. I noticed that the defense has petitioned the court to have the defendants' case heard in juvenile court. That motion is denied. Heretofore both defendants will be tried as adults."

The judge looked down at Jessica and DeCalia and their attorneys.

"Are both of you prepared to proceed?" she asked.

"Yes, your honor," Community Prosecutor Wellesley said.

"Yes, your honor," Stern said.

"There will be a fifteen-minute recess, and when we return, the jurors will be here, and the prosecution will begin its side of the case."

The judge slammed the gavel and rose from behind the bench.

****

DeCalia watched intensely as the twelve jurors sat in the jury box. There were three white men, five black women, two black men, and two white women. They all appeared to be over thirty.

Where are all the young jurors who live in DC? DeCalia wondered.

The prosecutor stood and walked close enough to the jury box that he could have touched a few jurors if he wanted to.

"Today, you'll hear about DC high school students —DeCalia Thomas and Jessica Barnes— who viciously and purposely attacked a fellow student, Tashera Odom. You'll hear how they approached Tashera Odom in broad daylight, surrounded her, and pounced on her as if they were animals in the jungle. You will see pictures of the injuries that Tashera Odom suffered at the hands of these young women—women she did not know and had never met until they approached her. If any of you has children, I want you to think about how you would feel if your child came home with the bruises, rib injuries, busted lips, and cuts that Tashera Odom had. Would you want your child's attacker to go free? I don't think so."

Jessica's lawyer, Harold Stern, stood and walked to the center of the courtroom.

"The prosecutor and I agree that Tashera Odom was viciously attacked. That is something I'm deeply sorry for. But who attacked Tashera Odom? There were three girls at the scene of the crime, and no witnesses that saw who did what. So, the prosecutor has decided to forget all the details and simply say these girls were there; they inflicted all of this pain and punishment on Tashera Odom. But where are the facts? Where is the witness who saw Jessica Barnes hit Tashera Odom? Where is the witness who saw DeCalia Thomas hit Tashera Odom? Where is the witness?" the attorney said and walked over to the juror's box. "Oh, I remember. The prosecution doesn't have one." Stern sat.

"Oh so what? I just beat myself up, is that it?" Tashera yelled from behind the prosecutor's table. DeCalia and Jessica turned in Tashera's direction, but lowered their eyes when her head turned toward them. The prosecutor looked at Tashera and shook his head trying to convey that she shouldn't be having an outburst. Detective Stewart walked over to Tashera and tapped her on the shoulder.

"Tashera, take a walk with me for a few minutes." Tashera and Detective Stewart walked just outside the doors of the hearing.

****

"Your honor, we call Detective Rodriguez to the stand," Community Prosecutor Wellesley said.

Detective Rodriguez raised her right hand and was sworn in. An assistant from the prosecutor's table brought in several boards with pictures of Tashera's bruises blown up to poster size.

"Did you take these pictures of Tashera Odom?" the prosecutor asked.

"Yes," Detective Rodriguez replied.

"What was the date and time?"

"We took the pictures on Monday April 2nd at about seven p.m."

The prosecutor walked over to a picture of a cut on Tashera's forehead.

"Explain what this is a picture of."

"It's a picture of Tashera Odom. It's the space just above her eyebrow.

"How long have you been on the force, Detective Rodriguez?"

"Eight years."

"In eight years, how would you rank this case—in terms of the injuries that the victim received?"

Detective Rodriguez returned her gaze to the pictures of Tashera.

"On a scale from one to ten—one being mild and ten being harsh?" Wellesley said.

Detective Rodriguez ran one finger across both brows. "It's definitely an 8."

"Thank you, Detective Rodriguez. We have nothing further for this witness."

"Defense, your witness," the judge said.

Langford Dempsey stood and adjusted the knot on his tie.

"Detective Rodriguez, when is the last time that you've seen Tashera Odom?"

"A couple of days ago," Detective Rodriguez said.

"Was she unconscious when you saw her?"

"No."

"Was she in a wheelchair or unable to walk?"

"No."

"When was the last time that you had a conversation with Tashera Odom?"

"Again, a couple of days ago."

"Was she coherent during your conversation?"

"Yes," Detective Rodriguez answered, annoyed.

"In your opinion, Detective Rodriguez, when you last saw and spoke with Tashera Odom, did she look as if she was suffering from life-threatening injuries?"

Detective Rodriguez looked at the pictures of Tashera that hung in the courtroom.

"It doesn't matter that she's healed fast."

Dempsey walked quickly to the witness booth.

"Answer the question, Detective."

"She still looks bad to me."

Dempsey rolled his eyes at Detective Rodriguez and walked to face the jury.

"But, the question is when you last saw and spoke with Tashera Odom, did she look as if she was suffering from life-threatening injuries?"

Detective Rodriguez ran her tongue across her front teeth.

"No," she replied in a mumbled voice.

"Detective Rodriguez, speak loud enough for the jury to hear you. What was your answer?"

"No," Detective Rodriguez said and inhaled.

"We have nothing further for this witness," Dempsey said and headed back to the defense table.

"You may be seated," the judge said.

Community Prosecutor Wellesley stood. "Your honor, we call Tashera Odom to the stand."

The bailiff walked to the door of the hearing room and opened it.

"It's your turn," Detective Stewart said.

Tashera walked slowly through the courtroom and looked over at DeCalia and Jessica. She knew if they hadn't jumped her, she could have whipped them both—easily—in a one-on-one.

As the bailiff swore Tashera in, Jessica and DeCalia doodled on their notepads.

"Tell us what happened on Monday, April 2—the day that you were attacked."

"I was walking home from the mini mart and three girls in hoodies and glasses came up to me out of nowhere."

"You didn't hear them approach you?"

"No, I was listening to my iPod."

"What happened when they approached you?"

"They started saying that they were gonna get me. They called me names, stuff like that."

"Then what did you do?"

"I looked around to see if there was a way that I could get away. I wanted to try to run as fast as I could."

"Did you try to run?"

"Yeah, but the shortest girl in the group, she tripped me and I fell."

"Shortest girl? What do you mean by that? I thought you couldn't identify your attackers."

"No, I didn't see their faces because of the dark glasses and the hoodies. But there was a chubby girl, a skinny girl, and a short girl. Chubby and Skinny are sitting over there," Tashera pointed to DeCalia and Jessica and rolled her eyes.

"Did you notice anything besides their body types?" the prosecutor asked.

"Yeah, the chubby one kicked me a lot, and she had on some Timberlands. I remember getting kicked in my ribs and looking up at whose legs those shoes belonged to. The girl with the fat thighs had fat feet, too, and they were wearing boots."

There was a low rumble of chuckles throughout the courtroom.

"Is there anything else you remember about that day?"

"Yeah, the fat girl knocked my Oatmeal Crème pie outta my hand, and it's obvious she didn't need it."

After another series of chuckles, the judge lowered her gavel and said, "Order in the court."

"We have nothing further for this witness," Wellesley stated.

"Defense witness," the judge said as Dempsey rose from his chair.

"I am very sorry for everything that has happened to you," Dempsey said.

Tashera looked Dempsey up and down.

"If you were so sorry, you wouldn't be representing those two winches."

Wellesley threw a look at Tashera and shook his head.

Tashera sat back in her chair.

"Miss Odom, you are to simply answer the questions that are asked of you. Do you understand?"

"Yes."

"Do you like Marion Barry High?"

"It's okay."

"If you were to grade the school, what grade would you give it?"

Tashera looked to the back of the courtroom and saw Mr. Ryland sitting by himself.

"I'd give it D."

"A D?" Dempsey frowned his face. "That's not an okay grade. Why would you give Marion Barry High a D?"

"It's too much violence in our school."

"Violence like when you were jumped?"

"Yes."

"Would you say that you have a lot of friends at school?"

"No."

"Why?"

"Because people talk too much, and there's too much jealousy, I don't have any parts of that."

"Do you know the defendants?"

"No."

"Does it make sense to you that the defendants would have attacked you, a person that they didn't know?"

"No, it doesn't make sense, but it still happened."

"In your previous testimony you mention seeing someone skinny, someone fat, and someone short attack you. But there are millions of people that fit those descriptions in this area. That's not a definitive description of your attackers."

Tashera starts to look at her fingernails.

"When you were attacked, do you remember seeing Jessica Barnes?" Dempsey asked while pointing to Jessica.

"No, but I told you they were wearing hoodies and glasses."

"Just answer the questions, please. Did you see Jessica Barnes' face when you were jumped?"

"No."

"Did you see DeCalia Thomas' face when you were attacked?"

"No."

"So in all honesty, you didn't see the faces of your attackers. According to your eyewitness account, somebody else could have attacked you, couldn't they?"

"Well, if I was the only eyewitness and there was no such thing as DNA, maybe. But, those girls did it and you know it..."

"Objection!" Dempsey said. "Objection."

Tashera looked at the Community Prosecutor who fought back a sly smile.

"We have nothing further for this witness," Dempsey said and sat.

"You can be seated, Ms. Odom," the judge said.

"Let's take this time to have an hour recess for lunch," the judge said. "We'll reconvene in sixty minutes."

****

The police escorted Jessica and DeCalia to a holding area while Harold Stern went looking for Lenise Barnes. He led her outside in front of the courthouse.

"Ms. Barnes," he said, "I don't know how much you understand about court cases, but that didn't go well. We need to sever Jessica's ties from DeCalia immediately before this situation spirals out of control."

"She doesn't want to," Lenise replied. "She wants to be loyal or stupid—whatever it is."

"Jessica is still sixteen and though she is being tried with DeCalia as an adult, you can petition the court for her as a minor and act on her behalf. If she were being charged by herself for a first-time offense, she would not even be charged as an adult. Based on the victim's testimony, the person that she saw inflict the most damage on her is DeCalia. If we separate them, I feel Jessica would be looking at probation alone. She may even be able to get her juvenile record sealed, and none of this will ever come to light again."

"What about the other girl?"

"You need to get your daughter as far away from her as possible."

"What can I do?"

"We can write up a petition to sever."

"Are you sure this will help Jessica?"

"Yes."

"Okay," Lenise Barnes said.

"I'll have one of my assistants bring the petition over. When we return from lunch, we'll petition to sever."

Chapter 37

As the lawyers and reporters began to spill back into the courtroom, Tashera tugged her mother's arm.

"I want to go home," Tashera said.

"I need to stay so I can hear what them li'l hussies gotta say," Sheila said.

"Ima catch the metro then."

Tashera was anxious to get home so that she could see if she'd received an email from the schools that she'd applied to—even a confirmation that her application had been received would have been a relief. Ahmed had reassured her that the schools would respond quickly to her since they had already offered him a scholarship. She checked her voicemail just before she got on the Metro and none of the schools had called her.

****

Shortly after the judge entered the courtroom, Harold Stern requested permission to approach the bench.

"Your honor," he said, "Lenise Barnes, the mother of sixteen-year-old Jessica Barnes has requested for her daughter's case to be severed from DeCalia Thomas' case."

The judge put her hand over the microphone that stood before her.

"We need to go to my chambers to discuss this," she said. "Bring her mother with you."

"Court will be adjourned until tomorrow," the judge said into the microphone and then slammed down her gavel.

227

Something is wrong, DeCalia thought. Behind the defense table, DeCalia leaned toward Jessica.

"What is going on?" she asked. "What did your lawyer tell the judge?"

"I don't know," Jessica said.

Jessica looked back at her mother and mouthed, "What is going on?"

Lenise looked away from her daughter.

The bailiff came and took DeCalia out of the courtroom and then an assistant to the bailiff removed Jessica.

****

Attorney Stern put a packet of papers on the judge's desk.

"I see this is your motion to sever," the judge said. "Ms. Barnes, what took you so long to decide on this course of action?"

"My daughter didn't want to be separated from her friend."

"That wasn't the best decision for your daughter even though that's what she wanted. Sometimes parents have to make decisions for their children—that's why God gave children parents."

The judge started to flip through the papers.

"Has Jessica ever had any other problems with the law?" the judge asked.

"No," Lenise Barnes said.

"Has she had problems in school?"

"No."

"I'm going to order this case to be moved to family court."

"Thank God," Lenise Barnes said and smiled at the judge.

As Lenise left the judge's chambers, she thought about Jessica. Yes, she would be devastated to learn that Lenise had her case severed from DeCalia's, but in the end, Lenise had to think about her daughter.

With Jessica's case being moved to family court, she wouldn't face hard time.

In the end, for Lenise, it didn't matter who started this tragic event; the only thing that mattered was her daughter's life.

If that meant that DeCalia would face the harshest penalties alone, so be it.

Chapter 38

Friday, April 13
Eleven days after the attack

The second day of the trial started as DeCalia sat behind the defense table without her friend Jessica. She had her attorney on the right side and one of the attorney's assistants on the left side, but she felt alone without Jessica beside her. When she first walked into the courtroom, she looked around for familiar faces. Her brother smiled at her, her mother frowned at her, and Mr. Ryland simply nodded.

After the judge entered the courtroom, the prosecution began with its case.

"We're continuing this case against DeCalia Thomas," the prosecutor stated. "We'd like to call Dr. Elliot to the stand."

Dr. Elliot entered the courtroom, sat in the witness box, and was sworn in. An assistant from the prosecutor's table pushed the large photos of Tashera's injuries so that the poster-sized images faced the jury.

"Dr. Elliot, did you treat Tashera Odom on the day in question?"

"Yes."

"What did you diagnose?"

"She had facial lacerations, bruised ribs, and internal bleeding to some of her reproductive organs."

There was a silence that dropped over the courtroom.

"Can you point to the photos that reflect what you're talking about?"

Dr. Elliot pointed to four different photos that reflected the cuts on Tashera's face and the bruised skin that shielded her ribs.

"Didn't you say that she had reproductive organ damage as well?"

"Yes, but those are x-rays. You don't have them displayed here," Dr. Elliot said.

"Well, explain to us, Dr. Elliot, what the internal injuries were?"

"Around her uterus and fallopian tubes, there was internal bleeding. The muscles around those organs tore."

"Is that a grave condition?"

"Yes, because it impacts a woman's ability to have children."

"Will Tashera Odom be able to have children?"

"Maybe not, we really don't know yet," Dr. Elliot said.

One of the female jurors in the front row let out a gasp.

"From your examination, could you tell what kind of situation would cause that kind of injury?"

"Poking with an instrument, kicking with a hard shoe or boot, and even punching directly in the lower abdomen."

"Did you say kicking?"

"Yes, I did."

"Thank you, Dr. Elliot."

"Defense?" the judge said.

"We have nothing for this witness, your honor."

"Dr. Elliot, you can step down now."

"The prosecution would like to call Ashe Thurgood to the stand," Wellesley said as he stood.

Ashe walked to the witness box wearing his paramedic's uniform. After he was sworn in, he answered several questions by the prosecutor.

"How did you meet Tashera Odom on Monday, April 2nd?"

"I was looking out a window, and I saw three girls shouting, flailing their arms, and moving in a circle. I couldn't tell from where I was standing exactly what they were doing, so I ran over to them."

"What did you find once you got there?"

"Three girls were beating up a girl who was lying on the ground."

"Beating up? What do you mean by beating up?"

"One girl was kicking her, and the other girls were shouting obscenities."

"When you walked up to the scene who did you see kicking Tashera?"

Ashe pointed at DeCalia and said, "DeCalia Thomas."

"Jury, please note that the witness just identified DeCalia Thomas."

"What happened next?"

"I flashed my badge and told them to get away from the victim. They backed away and got into a car, and I started helping Tashera."

"Was she conscious when you started helping her?"

"No. I started talking to her. I propped her head up and started to check for the types of injuries she had. I called 911 immediately so she could be taken to the hospital."

"What do you think would have happened if you hadn't come to help her?"

"Objection!" The defense attorney said. "Calls for speculation."

"Do you remember what the girls who were attacking Tashera were wearing that day?" Wellesley asked.

"They all had on black hoodies and sneakers, except for DeCalia. She had on the yellow Timberland boots."

"How do you know what kind they were?"

"I own the exact same pair."

"While you were there did you hear any of the girls call each other by name?"

"One of the girls called DeCalia 'Calia'. I didn't hear anyone else mention any names."

"Thank you, Mr. Thurgood."

"Defense?" the judge said.

"We have nothing for this witness," Dempsey said.

"Mr. Thurgood, you're excused."

Detective Stewart took the stand next. He strolled to the jury box like he'd been there a million times before.

"How are you affiliated with this case, Detective Stewart?"

"I lead the investigation—meaning I interviewed the victim, the defendant, and the witness. I collected evidence on the case."

"Evidence? What evidence did you collect?"

"I collected a black sweatshirt and bloody boots from DeCalia Thomas' home."

"The prosecution would like to introduce this black sweatshirt into evidence," the prosecutor said as an assistant brought up the sweatshirt in a plastic bag, showed it to the judge, then to the defense table, and then back to Detective Stewart.

"Is this the sweatshirt?" the prosecutor asked.

"Yes," Detective Stewart replied.

"Tell us about the sweatshirt."

"It had dirt and element tracings embedded on it that were similar to the dirt and elements that exist in the vacant lot where Tashera was found."

"What does that mean to say a lay person?"

"It means that there's a great likelihood that DeCalia's sweatshirt was at the scene of the crime because each part of the city has its own unique make-up. The dirt tracings found in her shirt, you wouldn't have been able to get say from a parking lot near the Capitol."

"So we can assume if her sweatshirt was there, then she was there."

"That's what the evidence would suggest."

"The prosecution would like to introduce these boots into evidence," the prosecutor said as an assistant displayed the yellow Timberland books to the jury and the judge before placing them in front of Detective Stewart.

"So noted," the judge said.

"Are these the boots?" the prosecutor asked Detective Stewart.

Detective Stewart took the plastic bag. "Yes."

"Tell us about the boots," the prosecutor said.

"These are DeCalia Thomas' boots, and they had blood stains around the toe. The blood matched the DNA of Tashera Odom."

"What does this evidence suggest?"

"It suggests that at some time DeCalia Thomas' boots connected with Tashera Odom's DNA."

"Thank you. We have nothing further," Wellesley said and sat.

"Defense?" the judge said.

"Detective Stewart," Dempsey said as he approached the bench.

"Is it possible for students in the same school to have each other's DNA on their clothing, in their lockers, in their bookbags?"

"Yes, but…"

"*Yes* is sufficient," Dempsey said. "Is it possible for a girl to say have a nosebleed in the girls locker room, not clean it up, and then another girl come in that same locker room, step into the blood and get the DNA on her shoe?"

"It's possible."

"Is it possible that DeCalia could have worn her sweatshirt while walking across the vacant lot in question and picked up those element tracings on a day that Tashera Odom was not attacked? Is that possible?"

"Yes."

"Did you ever ask DeCalia Thomas had she been over in the area of the vacant lot prior to April 2nd?"

Detective Stewart looked down at his shoes and exhaled.

"No."

"I didn't think so. We have nothing further for this witness," Dempsey said.

Detective Stewart stood.

"The prosecution rests, your honor," Wellesley said.

Chapter 39

Tashera and Ahmed had been looking for Georgia apartments on the internet when her mother sent her a text message saying that she needed to return to court.

"Dag, I gotta go to court again," she said. "I'll be so glad when this is all over."

"I know, but we're getting close. You gotta admit it."

"It seems like I should be happy that the case is going on and the city is taking it seriously, but something seems wrong with my mom and my brother—they're acting differently all of a sudden."

"They probably just going through the same things you are. You shouldn't trip off of that."

"You're probably right."

"You want me to come to court with you?" Ahmed asked.

"Can you swing it?"

"For my main girl? I can swing anything."

"That's why I love you, Ahmed. You always got my back."

Ahmed and Tashera signed out of school at the front desk and hopped the metro to the courthouse.

****

DeCalia drew her name over and over again on her notepad, waiting for court to commence. The judge finally entered and began proceedings.

"The court has given permission for the defense to recall a witness to the stand," the judge said. "You may proceed."

DeCalia's attorney, Langford Dempsey, stood. "Defense would like to call Tashera Odom to the stand."

Tashera stood and Ahmed squeezed her hand. She looked down and smiled at him and walked to the witness box.

"Bailiff, would you please remove the defendant from the courtroom?"

The bailiff walked over to DeCalia and withdrew her from the courtroom.

Moments later, three people dressed in black sweats, hoodies, and sunglasses walked into the courtroom with their backs toward Tashera.

"Can you identify the defendant out of these three people?" the attorney asked.

Tashera looked confused. All of the women looked the same. "No, I don't know which one she is," Tashera said.

DeCalia, one of the women in black, looked up and locked eyes with a man who'd been sitting on the aisle next to Tashera's mother.

The man, Khalil imitated a gun with his fingers, pointed it directly at her, and pulled the trigger.

Li'l Tommy who'd been sitting behind DeCalia's table saw her eyes go wide and heard her breathing grow heavy. He looked over at Khalil as he put his hand back down.

"Ladies, turn to the side," Dempsey instructed.

"Ms. Odom, can you tell which one is the defendant from this angle?"

Tashera stared hard.

"The defendant is chickenhead number 2," Tashera said and smiled.

"Why have you selected number 2?" Dempsey asked.

"Because the shape of the bottom of number 2's leg is the same shape as the person who kicked me. I couldn't see her face, but I could see the bottom of her legs."

"Ladies," Dempsey said, "please remove your hoods now."

All three women removed their hoods, and DeCalia was the second in line.

"The defense rests, your honor." Dempsey walked back to his table with his head down. Tashera walked past the defense table and out of the courtroom.

"Let's adjourn twenty minutes before your closing arguments," the judge said and slammed her gavel.

****

Li'l Tommy exited the courtroom and called Nine Mill, one of the senior members of Deuce Five.

"Yo," Nine Mill said.

"It's LT."

"Whaddup?"

"I seen that dude—he's here."

"What you tryna do?"

"You know what it is. I'm on 4th Street in NW outside of the court building. It's too cold for me right now."

"I'll see you in ten minutes."

Li'l Tommy hung up and waited. Nine Mill had told Tommy that if he ever needed a gun, all he had to do was call him and tell him that it was cold. Nine Mill would bring him the heat he needed to take care of any situation.

Nine Mill pulled up in a Honda Accord with tinted windows. He handed Tommy a Glock .357 wrapped in a camouflage bandana.

"That's what's up," Tommy said and shook Nine Mill's hand.

"Keep it gangsta," Nine Mill said and pulled off.

****

DeCalia and Langford Dempsey convened in a conference room on the side of the courtroom. Mr. Ryland knocked on the door and entered.

"What were you doing out there, trying to send me to the electric chair?" DeCalia asked.

"Langford, it looked pretty bad," Mr. Ryland said.

"We should probably go to the prosecutor and try to plead guilty," Dempsey said. "They'll probably give us less time that way. Juries can be brutal."

Mr. Ryland put his briefcase on the table and took out a report holder.

"Let's request a meeting with the prosecutor," he said. "I've put together a supervisory work release program. Students who've had disciplinary problems and trouble with the law will live in a dormitory like setting in Maryland. They'll be given jobs on the land; they'll be taught a foreign language. It's an opportunity to get the kids out of the negative environments in their neighborhoods."

"How did this come about?" Dempsey asked.

"I've been looking at real estate for years, but since this whole situation happened, I've been thinking about how I can help. Buying this building I found and housing the program there is what I can do."

"So when do you plan to get started?"

"I plan to buy the building in the next couple of weeks. I want DeCalia to be one of the first success stories from the program. I expect it to be up and running in six months. "

DeCalia looked up to Mr. Ryland. "Would it mean I wouldn't have to go back to Oak Hill?" she asked, her voice high and strained.

Mr. Ryland patted her shoulder as Dempsey looked over the paperwork.

"This looks good," he said. "I would prefer you be there at the meeting."

"For what?"

"Your name carries a lot of weight, and the prosecution would definitely consider brokering a deal with you headline worthy."

"Well let me know after you have the time set up."

"It'll probably be immediately after court's adjourned today."

Mr. Ryland slipped an arm over DeCalia's shoulder and squeezed it. "I'll stick around."

****

Khalil sat in the courtroom, ready for the trial to be over. He couldn't wait to find another girl soldier in Oak Hill to take DeCalia out. From the testimony, it seemed that DeCalia inflicted the most damage on Tashera. If he didn't find another young girl in Oak Hill to do the job, he'd planned on waiting for DeCalia to get out of Oak Hill. He'd stomp her himself if he had to.

He was glad with the way the case was going. There was no way the court would set DeCalia free.

****

"Let's proceed with the closing arguments," the judge said.

Community Prosecutor Wellesley rose from his chair.

"Your honor, I would like to request an emergency recess," Dempsey said.

"What for?"

240

"New developments from the defendant that I would like to share with the prosecutor."

"Okay. This case will resume tomorrow morning at nine. Court's adjourned," the judge said and banged the gavel.

Attorney Dempsey walked over to the prosecutor's table. "Can we talk now in the conference room?" he asked.

"I prefer the privacy of my office," Wellesley replied. "I'm going there now. Meet me in thirty minutes."

"I will."

****

Khalil and Sheila exited the courtroom utilizing the handicap ramp.

"Tashera couldn't wait to be up out of here," Khalil said.

"She's moving as soon as school is over," Sheila said.

"Movin'? Movin' where?"

"She's going to college away from here. She hates DC."

"I could never leave DC, and you know I gotta look out for you, Mom."

"I know. I know you'll be looking out for me."

As Sheila pushed Khalil's wheelchair toward the parking area, Li'l Tommy jumped out from behind a large blue mailbox and stood in front of Khalil. Li'l Tommy took the pistol from his right pocket and pulled the trigger. The bullet entered Khalil's brain.

Khalil's head hit the back of his wheelchair and with the last few seconds that he had left he thought about his life. He remembered when he could walk. He remembered fun times with his father. He remembered his sister as a little girl. He remembered coming home from the playground at three years old and running headfirst toward his mom and hugging her with all of his might. He realized that he wouldn't see his sister again. He realized that he wouldn't be able to help his mother. A tear rolled down his face, then his brain stopped.

"Khalil," Sheila screamed as Tommy ran off in the opposite direction.

"Oh God, Khalil," Sheila cried and hugged his head and shoulders as if her embrace would bring him back to life.

The ambulance came within a few minutes and pronounced Khalil dead on the scene. Sheila stood zombie-like when Khalil's body was put in the ambulance.

Would Khalil be in a wheelchair if you didn't live in Southeast? Sheila heard Richard's voice echo in her head. As the ambulance pulled off, Sheila trudged along 4th Street, aimlessly.

Would he be dead if I lived somewhere else? Sheila asked herself.

****

Attorney Dempsey and Mr. Ryland met Prosecutor Wellesley in his office.

"Wellesley, you remember Mr. Ryland, right?"

"Certainly."

"We want a plea bargain for DeCalia Thomas," Mr. Dempsey said.

"Why would I do that now? It's so clear that you are losing the case."

"Mr. Ryland is here because he's initiating a rehabilitative program for adolescents who have had discipline issues and problems with the law. We want DeCalia to be a part of that program."

Mr. Ryland put a copy of his proposal on the table and pushed it toward the prosecutor.

"What's in it for me?" Wellesley asked.

"Me and some of my friends from the NBA and other businessmen around the country are funding this project," Ryland replied. "It'll get a lot of media attention. We'll name you as one of the founding partners."

"How soon before it rolls out?"

"Six months. Nine tops," Ryland said.

"We're asking for a twelve-month stint at Oak Hill for DeCalia and another two years at the Ryland Center for Youth," Dempsey added. "It's a three-year sentence, but one that'll impact the defendant's life in a positive manner."

"Do you have some of your partners already outlined?" the prosecutor asked.

"Of course. I can't name names until everything is signed."

"I'll consider everything you have and let you know."

Mr. Ryland knew that without his clout and money, Prosecutor Wellesley wouldn't even consider his offer. Kids in the inner city didn't have a chance if people in high places weren't willing to fight for them. Mr. Ryland hoped that DeCalia wouldn't blow the opportunity to turn her life around.

Chapter 40

Monday, April 16
Fourteen days after the attack

Tashera stayed in the bed all day after her mother told her that Khalil had been gunned down. She cried uncontrollably and refused to eat. Her greatest fear of growing old without a brother had come true. Ahmed had been calling for the past two days and some of her former hair clients had called her cell phone as well. She refused to answer. She didn't feel like pretending that she was okay—that life was okay.

****

Sheila sat on the couch as if she was waiting for Khalil to wheel himself through the door. The past three days had been like living in a nightmare. Her cousin Richard had stopped by her house and brought food for her and Tashera. She'd eaten a little bit of potato salad, but she couldn't get down much else. She didn't have money to bury Khalil, and she didn't want to ask Tashera for her money. She knew Tashera had saved up a lot of money, but was planning to use it for college. The six hundred dollars that Sheila had in the bank wasn't enough to buy Khalil a decent casket.

****

Mr. Ryland, DeCalia, and Attorney Dempsey met with the prosecutor.

"I've decided to accept the plea agreement," Wellesley said. "DeCalia Thomas will serve twelve months in Oak Hill and then two years with the Ryland Center for Youth Program," the prosecutor said.

"Man, that's three years," DeCalia said and frowned.

"You were facing ten to twenty. You don't want to go back and face that jury, do you?" Attorney Dempsey asked.

DeCalia thought about the last two weeks of her life. In less than 14 days, her whole world had changed and Oak Hill was a painful, negative part of that time.

She knew a year at Oak Hill would feel like being in a maximum-security prison. And she knew Ryland would never allow her to forget this mistake. And she also knew that she really didn't want to forget.

She, Jessica and Alexandra could have permanently damaged Tashera. It's only but for the grace of God that they all didn't face murder charges.

"No," she said, her voice soft, "I don't."

"I didn't think so."

****

Ahmed drove over to Tashera's house and rang the doorbell. Sheila answered the door with her usually fly hair matted down like a cheap rug.

"Hello Ms. Odom. Is Tashera here?"

Sheila just opened the door, sat back on the couch, and stared at the television. When Ahmed opened Tashera's bedroom door, he saw her lying on her side, sobbing quietly.

Ahmed sat on the bed next to her. "You gotta get up and walk around," he said to her.

"I don't feel like it."

"Look, my mom got me this new phone. I can check the internet and email on it," Ahmed said. "Let's check the internet for apartments in Atlanta at least. You should hear something about the schools soon. I'm really feeling Georgia Tech right now. That whole Atlanta vibe got me open."

Tashera held the phone in her hands, staring at it blankly. "Well go 'head then," she said, "'cause I'm not feeling it."

"Oh, so you're backing out on me now? That wasn't the deal. You said we'd go together if I found a way and now you're backing out? That ain't right."

"What are you talking about? My brother died. I don't want to think about school. I don't even want to go to school anymore!"

"Is that what you think Khalil would want for you? For you to sit up in this room and die and not pursue your dreams? That makes no sense, Tashera. He's probably somewhere right now wishing that you'd get out of bed, get out and do something. I don't recall him ever just sitting in his wheelchair not doing anything, do you?"

"Shut up, Ahmed! Just shut up."

"I'll be downstairs when you're ready," Ahmed said before leaving the room.

****

Richard King had received a call from the prosecutor's office saying that they'd drop the charges against Sheila Odom for the alleged attack on Anita Thomas. It was good news, but it wouldn't bring Khalil back, so Sheila probably wouldn't even care about it. Sheila's job was still in limbo, and he knew she'd need extra money in order to pay for Khalil's burial expenses. Richard decided he'd take a trip to Laurel Hospital and pay Sheila's boss a visit.

He had managed to keep his anger in check when the secretary told him that he had to wait to speak with Mr. Kotowsky. After almost fifteen minutes, he could no longer play Mr. Nice Guy.

Richard walked to the secretary's desk and leaned down.

"Listen," he said, "I'm the attorney representing Sheila Odom. I need about ten minutes of your boss' time. If he can't give me the time before we initiate this lawsuit, his boss is gonna make him wish he did. Why don't you pass that message along?"

The secretary picked up the phone and seconds later, Mr. Kotowsky opened up the door.

"Mr. King, how can I help you today?" he asked.

"Actually, it'll be more like how can I help you," Richard said and walked into the office. After sitting before Mr. Kotowsky's desk, Richard added, "I understand that you've suspended my client."

"We have strict off-the-job expectations of conduct for our employees—especially our supervisors."

"What are you basing your belief that Sheila Odom didn't meet those expectations?"

"It's a matter of public record, and we have some additional information."

"Don't bluff me, Mr. Kotowsky."

"I'm not bluffing. A lady called the hospital and said that she was being harassed by Sheila. That with all of the details in the *Washington Post*—clearly that was grounds to believe misconduct was occurring," Mr. Kotowsky said.

"The court just threw out the case from the lady who probably called your office. After all of these years that Sheila has worked for this hospital—without incident—it's shocking to me that you never thought to give her the benefit of the doubt. You took the word of a stranger over your own employee. I can tell you now that the lady who called you was, more than likely, lying."

Mr. Kotowsky's face paled.

"Mr. Kotowsky, I'm here because I fully intend on talking my client out of suing you. Now, she probably could sue and we'd probably win, but right now she's mourning the death of her son who was murdered three days ago."

"I didn't know."

"How could you? You're too busy listening to complete strangers and not taking the time to get to know your employees. This is my suggestion. I think you and this hospital should put together a benevolence fund for Sheila. It should be a minimum of twenty thousand dollars. This benevolence fund will help her pay to bury her son. You can see how that might be needed, right?"

Mr. Kotowsky looked willing to say yes on the spot. He nodded and said, "Continue."

"You and this hospital should give her another ten days off—with pay—so that she can mourn her son properly. And with all of your generosity, I'll encourage my client not to sue you for suspending her without cause, causing emotional stress and duress, and a host of other issues that I could potentially add on to her lawsuit. When you're done thinking it over, you can send a letter of reinstatement and a check payable to Sheila Odom to the address on my business card. If I were you, I wouldn't take longer than 48 hours."

Richard King stood and extended his hand to Mr. Kotowsky. "Thanks for your time."

****

Jessica, her mother, and her attorney sat in family court while the judge reviewed her case. Because she didn't have any other bad marks on her record, she was given probation and sent home. Jessica knew that she'd received the least punishment of DeCalia and Alexandra though the whole attack was her idea. The guilt that she felt made looking in the mirror barely possible.

****

Still lying upon her bed, Tashera turned her head and stared at Ahmed's cell phone. She sighed before grabbing it, opening it, and pushing enough buttons until she was able to open her email account.

She heard a knock at her door, and then she saw Ahmed peek his head inside.

She looked at him and rolled her eyes. "You still here?" she asked.

"I'll never let you push me away," Ahmed said and leaned against the doorjamb. "Besides," he added as a smile lifted his lips, "you still got my phone."

Tashera looked at Ahmed and shook her head.

"You're a mess," she said.

In her inbox, Tashera found an e-mail from Yasmin Shiraz and an email from Georgia Tech. An author responding to her could only be good news, Tashera thought. So she clicked on the e-mail from Yasmin first.

TASHERA,

THANKS FOR REACHING OUT TO ME. FIRST, I HOPE THE POLICE AND THE PROPER AUTHORITIES HAVE GOTTEN INVOLVED IN YOUR CASE. NOBODY SHOULD BE ATTACKED AND THE CASE GO WITHOUT PUNISHMENT. SECOND, IT TROUBLES ME THAT YOU ARE WALKING AROUND WITH A KNIFE. IF YOU CHANGE WHO YOU ARE, THEY WIN. I WOULD RATHER YOU CHANGE YOUR SCHOOL OR CHANGE YOUR NEIGHBORHOOD. CHANGING YOUR PERSONALITY CAN MAKE YOU MISERABLE FOR THE REST OF YOUR LIFE.

CAN YOU CHANGE SCHOOLS? IS THERE A RELATIVE OR GOD-PARENT THAT YOU CAN GO TO FOR THE LAST FEW MONTHS OF SCHOOL? CAN YOU FINISH SCHOOL EARLY? IF YOU'RE CLOSE TO FINISHING, YOU MIGHT WANT TO CONSIDER TAKING THE GED TO GET OUT OF THERE EARLY. IN CERTAIN SITUATIONS, GETTING OUT OF A NEGATIVE SITUATION IS BETTER THAN STAYING.

HAVE YOU AND YOUR PARENTS EVER TALKED ABOUT MOVING OUT OF THE NEIGHBORHOOD? SOMETIMES PARENTS THINK THE KIDS LIKE WHERE THEY LIVE AND SO THEY STAY FOR THEIR KIDS' SAKE. IF YOU DON'T LIKE IT, TELL YOUR PARENTS.

DO YOU HAVE A JOB? I'M ASKING BECAUSE SOMETIMES YOU CAN HELP YOUR PARENTS WITH SOME OF THE FINANCIAL STRAIN OF MOVING BY HAVING YOUR OWN RESOURCES. KIDS GROW UP THINKING THAT THEY ARE TO RELY ON THEIR PARENTS FOR EVERYTHING, BUT WHEN YOU CAN BE OF ASSISTANCE TO YOUR PARENTS, YOU SHOULD BE. IF YOU WANT TO MOVE (WHICH I THINK WOULD BE GREAT), LET YOUR MOM KNOW THAT YOU'LL HELP PAY FOR A MOVING VEHICLE OR HELP PUT MONEY DOWN ON THE DEPOSIT. YOUR PARENTS WILL REALLY SEE HOW MUCH YOU'RE MATURING WITH THIS TACTIC.

IN MY WORKSHOPS, I TALK A LOT ABOUT CHOICES IN LIFE, BUT I'M LEARNING MORE AND MORE THAT IT'S HARD TO MAKE POSITIVE CHOICES WHEN YOU'RE SURROUNDED BY NEGATIVITY. BY THE TONE OF YOUR LETTER, I FEEL THAT YOU'RE LOSING HOPE. DO AS MUCH AS YOU CAN—TALK TO TEACHERS WHO ARE HELPFUL, GUIDANCE COUNSELORS, PRINCIPAL, PROGRAM DIRECTORS, YOUR BOYFRIEND'S MOM, WHOEVER—TALK TO SOMEONE ABOUT WHAT YOU'RE FACING. AND, GO TO THEM WITH YOUR IDEA OF A SOLUTION. BELIEVE IT OR NOT, KIDS AND ADULTS ARE BOTH LOOKING FOR SOLUTIONS. IF THE RIGHT SOLUTION COMES, SOMEBODY IS

GONNA TAKE ADVANTAGE OF IT. THE WORST THING YOU CAN DO FOR YOURSELF IS SIT BACK AND DO NOTHING.

YOU ARE STRONGER THAN YOU REALIZE. DO SOMETHING.

YOUR GIRL,

Yasmin Shiraz

Ahmed continued standing by the opened door as Tashera jumped up and grabbed some clothes out of her dresser.

"So, you're finally up?" Ahmed asked.

Over her shoulder, Tashera rolled her eyes at him before taking the cell phone with her and heading into the bathroom.

She decided that she would get dressed for the first time in three days. She couldn't wallow in her room forever. She couldn't let everything that had happened beat her.

When Tashera stepped out of the bathroom, she closed the cell phone and hugged Ahmed.

"Let's go to your house for a while," she said.

Ahmed's eyes widened and a small smile flitted across his face. "Really?

"Yeah." Tashera offered him a slight smile in return, her first in days. "We got some plans to make for Atlanta."

Making Peace: Tips on Conflict Management

Steps to Managing Conflict

Understand your own feelings about conflict. This means recognizing your triggers—words or actions that immediately cause an angry or other emotional response. Your trigger might be a facial expression, a tone of voice, a finger being pointed, a stereotype, or a certain phrase. Once you know your triggers, you can improve control over your reactions.

Practice active listening. Go beyond hearing only words; look for tone, body language, and other clues to what the other person is saying. Pay attention instead of thinking about what you're going to say next. Demonstrate your concentration by using body language that says you're paying attention. Looking at the ground with your arms crossed says your uninterested in what the other person is telling you. Look the other person in the eye, nod your head, keep your body relaxed and your posture open.

Come up with suggestions for solving the problem. Many people can think of only two ways to manage conflict—fighting or avoiding the problem. Get the facts straight. Use your imagination to think up ways that might help resolve the argument.

Moving Toward Agreement

> ➢ Agree to sit down together in a neutral place to discuss the problem.
> ➢ Come to the discussion with a sincere willingness to settle the problem.

> ➤ State your needs—what results are important to you—and define the problem. Talk about issues without insulting or blaming the other person.
> ➤ Discuss ways of meeting needs or solving the problem. Be flexible and open-minded.
> ➤ Decide who will be responsible for specific actions after reaching agreement on a plan. Write the agreement down and give both people a copy.

Confronting the Issue

Good communication skills are a necessity throughout our lives. They allow us to resolve issues before they become problems and help keep us from getting angry. When talking to people, especially those who are confrontational, you should

> ➤ look and feel relaxed.
> ➤ keep your voice calm.
> ➤ be direct and specific about what's bothering you. Use "I" statements—statements that emphasize how you feel, rather than blaming the other person. Instead of yelling, "You always interrupt me. You don't care what I think," try saying "I feel frustrated when I can't finish making my point. I feel as though my opinions don't matter."
> ➤ ask—don't demand. Instead of saying, "Get away from me," try asking "Would you please leave me alone right now? I'm trying to talk to my friends?"
> ➤ make your statement once then give it a rest. Don't repeat your point endlessly.

If You Can't Work It Out, Get Help

Mediation. Many schools offer programs that train students to act as mediators for their peers. Mediators do not make decisions for people—they help people make their own decisions. Mediators encourage dialogue, provide guidance, and help the parties define areas of agreement and disagreement.

Student Courts. Many schools have implemented teen courts to help students solve disputes. Teens serve as judges, juries, prosecutors, and defenders in each case. Students caught fighting on campus can use the courts to settle arguments, and teen juries can "sentence" those students to detention or community service, rather than imposing suspension or expulsion.

Anger Management. How to recognize attitudes, actions, and circumstances that trigger an angry reaction and how to control that reaction are skills that many teens—and even some adults have not learned. Anger management training helps individuals take command of their emotional reactions instead of allowing their emotions to take command of them.

Arbitration. In arbitration, a neutral third party determines an action. Disputing parties agree on an arbitrator who hears evidence from all sides, asks questions, and hands down a decision.

Where to Find Help

➤ Community or neighborhood dispute resolution centers
➤ Local government—family services
➤ Private organizations listed in the telephone directory's Yellow Pages under "arbitration" or "mediation services"
➤ Law school legal clinics

RETALIATION

This information was provided by the National Crime Prevention Council: 1000 Connecticut Avenue, NW, Washington, DC 20036 www.ncpc.org.

My Thank You's

I would like to thank the holy spirit for dropping these literary jewels into my soul and giving me purpose in my life.

I would like to thank my husband for believing in me and being a true partner in all of my endeavors.

I would like to thank my daughter and my son for making me laugh when I thought there was nothing to even smile about.

I would like to thank my parents and my family members for still welcoming me to Thanksgiving dinners and taking my phone calls.

My college friends- Shaconna, Buffy, and Stan- thank you for helping me grow. My girl, Monife, for being about the work for youth and helping me in so many ways, including providing the fertile soil for this story.

My soldiers for youth across the country: I love you and appreciate you. My crew at Planned Parenthood, Girls Inc., The Boys & Girls Clubs, Girl Scouts, SHINE, and the numerous independent organizations that make a difference every day.

Readers, Leaders in the book industry and Members of my network: I love and appreciate you. Brandon M, author extraordinaire, Laina in Boston, Eldorado in CT, Shon, the editor, Sara in PA, The Ford sisters, Locksie & ARC, Carvelas, Tiah & DC Bookman, Hakim & Black & Noble Books, Gordon & Afriqiah, Vanesse in Philly, Katina in DC, Nicole in LA by way of Syracuse, Dackeyia my coach, Carla the Editor, Ron at Mosaic, Yasmin at APOOO, Clarence at BIBR, Neal in DC, Janice in DC, Dr. K, Dr. Benjamin, Gwen in Florida, Bryant in Clemson, Pat at the Millennium Seat Pleasant Club, Charreah at Howard, Greg my Finance Man, Todd B at PGC, Justine at PGC,

Angelique in Philly, Kelly in Jacksonville, Jean my librarian, Shida in NYC, Shana at BIG in DC, Tion in Milwaukee, Tracy at Stanford, Joyce in ATL, Kevin in DE, Janice in DC, Lisa in San Francisco, Candice the Author, Krys in ATL, Lee & Radioscope, Karibu, Coast2Coast Readers, Marina in NYC, Vanesse in Philly, Demetrius in Richmond, Aharon in Richmond, Jiwe, Dorrie in VA, E. Monique in ATL, Tosha in LA, Lisa in Pink World, Gladys in Hampton, Michelle in Philly, Stephanie in Jersey, Yonder in MD, Val in Dayton, Vincent in TX, Tracy in LA, Delta Sigma Theta chapters nationwide, Bernice in VA, Clashous in FL, Sean at Borders, Tee in ATL, Curtis at NBCC.

If there is anyone that I've forgotten, charge it to my head and not my heart. Everyone who has been down for the cause, we are one in the journey.

Yasmin Shiraz

Discussion and Bookclub Questions

1. Tashera was originally an easy-going 17 year old. How do you feel the attack changed her emotionally? How do you think she'll relate to other women as she gets older? What helped Tashera get through this bad situation the most?

2. It's often said, "What goes around, comes around." Do you think Tashera's attack punished Ahmed for the way <u>he</u> treated Jessica?

3. Girls often fight other girls over boys. How does Jessica's attack on Tashera compare?

4. The central theme in this book is retaliation. Almost every character retaliates in some way. Discuss how each character retaliates in the book. Discuss how the situation would have been different had they acted differently instead of retaliating.

5. Sheila's husband wanted the family to move before he died. And, even after Khalil was paralyzed, Sheila still didn't move. Why do you think Sheila didn't move the family?

6. Khalil was paralyzed as a result of a robbery gone bad with his crew. Even so, he didn't leave the gang lifestyle behind. Why didn't he?

7. Violence is popularized in film and in music. Do you think Shiraz sensationalized violence in this story or spoke to real issues?

8. What other elements could have been added to the story in Retaliation?

9. If you wrote a letter to a famous person and asked them for advice, who would you write to and what would you ask them?

10. Even though he knew Jessica was in danger, Ahmed didn't want to go to the police. What would you do if you were in the same situation? Whose side did you take? Ahmed's or Mike's?

11. Sheila was angry when her only daughter was jumped, but her actions created other problems. How could she have reacted to help Tashera and get the case solved? How did Sheila's past affect her actions?

12. DeCalia and Alexandra supported Jessica when she wanted to jump Tashera. How do you feel Jessica and DeCalia's relationship is now that DeCalia is in jail and Jessica isn't? Could any of your friendships withstand a situation like this?

13. Mr. Ryland could have easily kept his millions and stayed away from a school like Barry High. Why do you think he really cared and decided to spend his time there? How would inner city schools change if more affluent African Americans invested in the schools?

14. Detective Stewart had to do his job, but how do you think he felt about seeing Tashera and Jessica in the hospital, Alexandra dead, and DeCalia in jail? Society often paints policemen as uncaring

individuals. How does Detective Stewart live up to this stereotype?

15. Richard defended Sheila even though he didn't have to and he knew she didn't really like him or respect him. What should Sheila have learned from Richard helping her? How does their family dynamic relate to yours?

16. Ahmed was willing to sacrifice his school choice so that he could help Tashera out of her situation. How does this idea relate to modern teen relationships?

17. Jessica has to live with knowing that her influence was the key reason that DeCalia was in jail and the impetus behind Alexandra going over the edge. Do you think her guilt is a worse punishment than going to jail? How could she have been punished differently?

18. Tashera loved spending time with her brother when he wasn't with the gang, how do you think she'll get over his death?

19. Society often puts brothers in a protective role. If society was different, do you think Khalil would have felt so strongly to avenge Tashera's attackers?

20. Li'l Tommy wanted to stand up for his sister, similar to Khalil. How could they have both stood up for their sisters without these consequences? Were either of their actions worth it? Why or why not?

Questions & Answers with
Yasmin Shiraz

1. Is *Retaliation* a true story?

No, but it is inspired by my work with youth and watching news that depicts life in the inner cities across America.

2. Who do you want to read *Retaliation*?

Everybody! I want teens to read it because I want them to see the whole side of the story. I want adults to read it to see how their actions impact some people. Sometimes we react to certain situations and we only see our own point of view. I wrote *Retaliation* so that all sides could see how violence impacts the community.

I especially want adults who come in contact with youth to read it—whether you're a parent, a teacher, or a member of law enforcement. There is a certain level of frustration that I sense when working with my young people. I don't feel that the average adult understands their frustration or wants to. It's unfortunate because adults are in positions to be helpful.

3. Why was it important to write *Retaliation*?

I needed to write a book that spoke on violence in our community because it is so prevalent and it is hurting and killing so many people. I'm at a point in my life where I make a conscious effort to do what matters.

4. The setting of Retaliation is in an urban community but violence is all over. What do you think society on a whole can do to curtail violence?

We have to talk to our youth about violence before they become the perpetrators or the victims. We have to become more visual in our stance against violence. Violence has to become unacceptable in all communities.

5. What's the hardest part about being a writer?

Making sure that you maintain your voice. In America, we live in a bandwagon culture. Whatever is hot, that's what everybody wants to jump on. I want to write about the things that are closest to my heart – whether they are popular or not.

6. What's the best thing about being a writer?

Being able to share your opinions, your perspectives and your hopes with people is the best thing. To know that something that you've written has inspired someone's life is truly awesome.

7. Do you have any advice for aspiring writers?

Listen to yourself. Listen to your concerns. Write about the things that move you and that keep you up at night. Don't worry about format at first. Just pick up a pen and start writing what you feel.

Sources

Page 39 & 83
The Blueprint for My Girls: How To Build A Life Full of Courage, Determination & Self-Love by Yasmin Shiraz (Simon and Schuster, 2004)

Pages 252-255
Making Peace: Tips on Conflict Management (National Crime Prevention Council)

About the Author

Yasmin Shiraz is the author of five other books, including the best selling *Blueprint* empowerment series. She conducts workshops and empowerment programs across the country. She's the creator of the Blueprint Empowerment Talks, How To Get into the Entertainment Business Tour, Get Your Hustle On: Entrepreneurship 101, and the Retaliation Townhalls. She can be heard on her radio show, Culturally Speaking with Yasmin Shiraz, which is available on I-Tunes. Additionally, Shiraz is the founder of The Signals Agency and Rolling Hills Press. Her website is: www.yasminshiraz.net.

Excerpt from
The Hive: A Novel
by Yasmin Shiraz

PROLOGUE

Night
Tuesday, January 9

It's 7:55 p.m. Rachel and Jada have hung a white sheet on Jada's wall that has written on it in red paint: WWW.DONTDATEAMENACE.COM.

"Are you almost ready?" Rachel asked as Jada put a blue pillowcase over her head with the eyes and mouth cut out. Rachel adjusted the webcam. They'd be streaming live video on their brand new website dontdateamenace.com in a matter of minutes.

Jada had taken off all of her jewelry and sat in a nondescript folding chair wearing all black, except for the blue pillowcase covering her head.

A bright light shone on Jada and she spoke—the webcam catching every moment.

"Tonight, I share my pain and hatred with you. There is a menace among us. At Elizabeth River High School, there is a guy whose photos are pictured on this website. He is spreading STD's, deadly STDs. Before you judge me, I am not doing this video to hurt anyone. I'm doing this because he's infecting people. I know this for a fact because he infected me...with not one but two sexually transmitted diseases.

"This guy is still dating girls in our school. He refuses to wear a condom. He will blackmail you, exert excessive force and do anything within his power to force you into having sex with him. This is absolutely true.

"So, when I first found out he gave me a disease, I thought about dying. I thought about killing myself. But then

I realized that wouldn't solve anything. It wouldn't prevent any of you from succumbing to the same fate as I have. This website is to prevent you from dating or being around a predator that will expose you to deadly diseases on purpose.

"Some of you will hate me for doing this. But I had to do something. I am going to out this person, little by little. I am going tell you which diseases I have been infected with. I don't know if what I am doing is legal. So, I hope you don't call the cops. I don't know if I can be arrested for revealing this person's identity, but somebody has to stop him. I figured it might as well be me.

"Right now, I know at least five girls at Elizabeth River High School are infected like me, but they don't know it. Over the next few days, I will reveal who you are. So, stay tuned."

Every few generations, music changes the way we live. Rock & Roll did it. Motown did it. Now, hip hop has done it...

FROM THE NATIONALLY ACCLAIMED PUBLISHER OF *MAD RHYTHMS* MAGAZINE

EXCLUSIVE

A Novel

YASMIN SHIRAZ

Ask for it wherever books are sold!

Own all Yasmin Shiraz books:

The Blueprint for My Girls: How To Build Life A Life Full of Courage, Determination & Self-Love (Simon & Schuster, $12.00)

The Blueprint for My Girls in Love: 99 Rules for Dating, Relationships & Intimacy (Simon & Schuster, $13.00)

The Blueprint Guide to Motivation & Success: Identify, Focus On & Achieve Your Goals (Herff Jones, $9.99)

**Exclusive: A Novel (Rolling Hills Press, $13.95)
Privacy: A Novel (Rolling Hills Press, $13.95)**

AVAILABLE ON: WWW.YASMINSHIRAZ.NET